Hope you enjoy
my family story
Dot Hatfield
March 2015

Also by Dot Hatfield

Every Day a New Day and other short stories

The Last to Know

To Find a Home

R.I.P Emma Lou Briggs

An Ordinary Day

A novel based on a true story

by Dot Hatfield

Alderson Press
Nashville

An Ordinary Day
A Novel based on a true story
By Dot Hatfield
ISBN: 978-0615927848

Also available in ebook format for the Amazon Kindle.

Published by
Alderson Press
2817 West End Avenue #126-168
Nashville TN 37203

For more information on titles by Dot Hatfield, visit
dothatfield.com

To Mother and Daddy
who each played a part
in this story.

An Ordinary Day

What is it that makes one day stand out from another? Why would one day be spectacularly happy and another tragic? Is it fate? Karma?

When Moses drove his sheep into the mountains on an ordinary day, he was not expecting to meet God in a burning bush. Or the morning Joseph donned his coat of many colors to show off to his brothers, he did not know he would end the day as a slave on his way to Egypt.

And so, when January 25, 1928 dawned clear and cold in peaceful Marietta, Oklahoma, no one in town had the slightest hint that before sunset on this ordinary day, someone they knew would die.

One

At dawn, two weeks after her sixteenth birthday, Anna Mae Long snuggled under warm quilts. Her younger sister slept soundly next to her. She sent a quick thought-prayer heavenward — her habit each morning on waking.

Thank You for another day.

As her mind formed the words of her morning prayer, a strange feeling of disquiet nudged her. She frowned, wondering about the uneasiness.

Is there something I forgot to do? She ran over the day's activities in her mind. *Today's Tuesday . . . Geometry homework done . . . basketball uniform washed and ironed for the game tonight.* She could think of nothing that might cause the odd hint of dread.

She'd been working daily on the memorization for the Epworth League's upcoming Bible Quiz. *"And we know that all things work together for good to them that love God and — and —" Something else, but I'll have it down by Sunday.*

Anna thought of a certain boy. *Monroe. I hope I get a*

letter today. I like him a lot. Does he like me back? He says he does. Is he serious? Or just a lady's man? Was it only a summer romance? It seemed more than that when I saw him at Christmas . . . And he writes nearly every week . . .

She rolled onto her back before stretching out her short frame, braced herself for the frigid sheets not warmed by her body. She inhaled deeply and held the cold air in her lungs for a few seconds before blowing her breath out in puffs. Small clouds of warm air drifted about the chilly room.

In the semi-darkness Anna smiled as she thought of how Mattie Lou had tried to teach her to blow smoke rings in the winter air. *I miss Mattie so much. Maybe that's the reason for this strange feeling.*

The Long family moved to Marietta four years ago. On Anna's first day in the new school, the teacher had seated her next to Mattie Lou Hudson. "Mattie, this is our new sheriff's daughter, Anna. Help her find her way around today."

From that moment the two girls were inseparable. They went everywhere together, often with Anna's younger sister, Johnnie Ruth, tagging along. They talked about boys, fixed each other's hair, practiced Charleston steps — in secret, because Mattie, a Baptist, was forbidden to dance. They were both stuck on Rudolf Valentino. When Mattie's dad died, Anna was there to hold her friend. Anna Mae Long knew the pain of losing a parent.

Then, last September, Mattie had to quit school to help her widowed mother. As much as Anna loved school, it wasn't the same without Mattie.

Maybe I'll drop by her house after she gets home from work. No, I can't. There's the basketball game. Well, tomorrow, then. Or the next day. I'll see her soon.

Cheered at the thought of spending time with her friend, Anna shook off the foreboding. *That was just my imagination. It's going to be a good day.*

She heard the cowbell on the back of the milk wagon as it made its way down Main Street. Stretching again, Anna reached out to shake Johnnie's shoulder.

"Wake up, Sleepyhead. Time to rise and shine."

Two

The Gaines' Dairy wagon ('Milk from Purebred Jersey Cows Since 1908') rattled down the street. The cowbell gave notice to wives and mothers inside the warm houses that fresh milk and butter would soon be left on their doorsteps. Wendell Allen tightened his muffler. He clicked at Beulah, wondering when Mr. Gaines would break down and buy a truck. Old Man Gaines contended that well-kept horses didn't freeze up in the winter nor boil over in the summer — more than he could say for most automobiles.

Wendell pulled up in front of the Eastham's two-story Victorian just as he saw their hired girl, Mattie Lou Hudson, half a block away, coming at a run. Wispy yellow curls escaped from her knitted hat, framing a pleasing face, rosy from the frosty air. Wendell hopped down from the wagon.

"You're late. Mrs. Eastham's gonna have your hide."

"You mind your business and I'll mind mine, Wendell

Allen. Wait right here till I get the empties."

She ran through the side yard to the kitchen door of the grand house. Frank Eastham, president of the Love County National Bank, was the closest thing Marietta had to a rich man. His wife was the only woman in town with full-time help.

Wendell stood shivering on the front walk, his ruddy cheeks mocking his sandy hair. Nothing said he had to wait around in freezing weather. It would serve Mattie right if he climbed back on the wagon and left. Folks were supposed to put their empty bottles out the night before.

But he stayed, so that Mrs. Eastham wouldn't have a reason to complain to Mr. Gaines about the milk wagon passing her by; so that Mr. Gaines wouldn't have an excuse to chew Wendell out; and so that Wendell would have a chance to see Mattie Lou's face one more time that day.

The first twelve years of his life, Wendell hardly knew Mattie Lou Hudson existed. He was in the fifth grade at the time, due to starting school late and being held back to repeat one year. One day at recess he and his friends were in a game of tree-tag when they heard a piercing scream come from the little kids' playground.

"She's dead! Help, somebody! She's dead!"

A tiny frame with a mass of yellow hair lay on the ground by the see-saw. Another little girl stood beside her, yelling her head off. One of the boys guffawed loudly.

They all knew that trick. Slide backward off the teeter-totter quickly while your partner is up in the air, giving him a quick ride to the ground.

The girl lying in the dirt didn't move. The other continued to scream. Wendell trotted over. He squatted beside the little blondie, lifted her up and set her on her feet. *Nothin but the wind knocked out of her.*

"You're okay," he said. The screamer hushed and the little girl caught her breath and began to cry. "Come on, now. You're okay. Everything's okay."

She wiped her tears with a dusty hand, creating a muddy streak across her face. Mrs. Ferrell came running up. "Come with me, Mattie Lou. Thank you, Wendell, you may go back to your playground now."

After that, Wendell noticed the little girl from time to time, sitting in church between her parents, walking downtown hand in hand with her daddy.

When Wendell laid out a couple of terms to help out on the farm, Mattie Lou began to catch up to him in school. By the time he was twenty and quit school for good, Wendell Allen noticed sixteen-year-old Mattie Lou Hudson often. But he never had occasion — or backbone — to speak to her. Until he saw her every morning bringing in the milk at the Eastham's house.

Now, Mattie walked toward him juggling three half-gallon containers.

"Did she get after you?"

"I told you to mind your business." Mattie blinked rapidly and sniffed a big sniff.

"Want me to spit in the milk?"

"Wendell!" Giggling, she looked up at him through still-wet lashes and favored him with a small grin.

If she ever gave him a big smile, he figured he would fall over and die from the beauty of it. He reached into the wagon and brought out two jugs and a pound of butter, the Eastham's usual order.

"A dozen of eggs also, please," Mattie Lou said softly.

Wendell counted out twelve eggs and carefully placed them in a brown paper bag.

"That's too much for you," he said. "You take the eggs and butter and I'll carry the milk."

At the kitchen door, Wendell took a deep breath. "You going to prayer meeting tomorrow night?"

"I suppose."

"How's about if I sit beside you and we share a hymn book?"

"It's a free country. Sit where you like."

"Awwwww. Mattie . . ."

"See you at church." She tossed her head, opened the screen door and slipped inside.

"That was a yes!" Wendell ran in place four or five

steps, then trotted back to the wagon. He patted the mare on the rump. "Old girl, I'll take that as a yes!"

He climbed up on the wagon and clicked at Beulah. The mare trotted down to the corner and turned on Creek Street. Hearing the bell, two women from the neighborhood, walked out into the cold morning.

"Howdy, Mrs. Beaver. Howdy, Mrs. McCarty," he called, pulling on the reins.

"Good morning, Wendell," Mary McCarty said. She crossed her arms, hugging herself against the cold wind. "Can we expect some sunshine today?"

"Yes'm. The Almanac says no more snow till February." He thought of Mattie Lou Hudson's shy smile, of the possibility of seeing her again tomorrow in church — maybe touching her soft hand behind the hymn book. His grin spread all over his face.

"It's going to be a wonderful day!"

Three

Mary McCarty placed the milk bottle in the old wooden box, pausing to watch a half-dollar-sized drop of melted ice fall into the tin pan below. She smiled as she reminded herself to put the card in the window so the ice man would come tomorrow. *That's the last block of ice I will ever need.* By Friday, her kitchen would be modern. By the end of the week, Sarah Eastham would no longer be the only woman in town with an electric refrigerator. Even though it cost almost as much as a car, Aaron was buying Mary a General Electric Monitor-Top.

Aaron McCarty, mayor of the city, might be called well-to-do. In Love County, farm implements and hunting rifles were considered necessities and McCarty's Hardware sold both.

But just because Aaron McCarty could afford an item, didn't mean he bought it. He could remember all too well the lack of money during the first years he was in business for himself. He wouldn't show off by living with personal luxuries his customers couldn't afford. The electric refrigerator for Mary was a big concession.

Mary took the biscuits out of the oven, placing them on the rack above the burners to stay warm. She cracked four eggs into the hot lard in the skillet. Lifting the butter dish and a jar of pear preserves from the top shelf of the icebox, she set them in the center of the table. She expertly scooped two eggs from the frying pan, put them on a plate and flipped the remaining eggs over in the grease. Sunny side up for Aaron, over hard for Olin.

Standing at the foot of the staircase, Mary called out, "Aaron, Olin — breakfast." She heard Aaron rap on the door of their son's bedroom and repeat her message.

Seventeen years old and set to graduate from high school in the spring, Olin was his parents' pride and joy. He worked in his papa's store every day after basketball practice. Mary would have wagered her new refrigerator that he had never tasted a sip of hard liquor. And girls? As far as his parents could see he showed no interest in the flappers with their short skirts and rolled down hose.

Aaron sat at the table in the spacious kitchen and opened the morning paper to the sports page. Olin bounded down the stairs, threw a leg over the chair back and plopped onto the bottom so hard the cane creaked.

Mary set his plate in front of him. "Now, don't wolf your breakfast, son. You have plenty of time."

"Looks real good, Mama." He washed down a huge bite of biscuit with a half glass of milk. "I might not be home for lunch."

"Oh? Why not?"

"Ask me no questions and I'll tell you no lies."

Aaron emerged from behind the newspaper. "What was that?"

"I'm sorry, sir. I was just joking."

Aaron lay the folded *Daily Oklahoman* beside his plate. He sprinkled an abundance of salt on his eggs.

"A fine game last night, Son. How many did you score?"

"Oh-h-h, I don't know. I wasn't counting."

Aaron's laughter boomed. "Well, you scored 23. I was very proud of you."

Pouring Aaron a coffee refill, Mary smiled at the exchange. She stopped to smooth Olin's cowlick. "What's this about you not eating lunch?"

"I need to go downtown at noon and buy a pencil. Mine is worn down to a nub and won't take another sharpening." Before Mary had a chance to answer Olin raced on. "Please, Mama. I really need some paper, too. And I'll come by the house and eat after I get them. I'll have time, I'm sure."

"Well, all right . . ."

Aaron looked at his son, a smile playing around his lips. "A pencil? Now, Son, I would have thought you could come up with a better line than that."

"Papa — "

"Am I supposed to believe you're going to miss your mama's cooking for a *pencil?* Come on, what's her name?"

"Papa!"

Mary laughed. "You boys stop teasing or someone's going to be late for school."

Chuckling, Aaron picked up his newspaper again.

Olin grabbed his cap and jacket. He fastened the slack in his pant leg with a clothespin. With a quick kiss for his mama, he hurried out the door and jumped on his bicycle.

Mary turned and wiped her hands on her apron. "You don't think he's really seeing a girl, do you?"

Aaron smiled. "Now, Mama, he's certainly old enough to be interested in girls. But he's too bashful to say boo to a goose."

"Maybe so. Will you be home for lunch?"

"I imagine. Floyd can watch the store. He's a good man." Floyd Hyde had come to work at McCarty's Hardware six months ago when business picked up enough to warrant it. A grown man nearing thirty with a wife and young baby, he was responsible and industrious. Certainly trustworthy enough to watch things while Mr. McCarty took a lunch hour.

"I'll see you about noon." Aaron pushed back from the table and took his hat and coat from the hall tree. He patted Mary's shoulder, kissed her forehead and struggled into his heavy overcoat.

Mary watched her husband back out the drive and head toward downtown. She gazed out her kitchen window as she washed dishes and reviewed her ordinary Tuesday. Beds to make and clothes to gather and take to Mrs. Potts for ironing. Olin's closet needed a good cleaning and outgrown items bagged for the Missionary Society's rummage sale. Wednesday was her day to have help with the house — Faye could work on Olin's closet tomorrow. Lunch would be ham sandwiches and brown beans cooked with the hock — maybe fried potatoes. The baking hen for supper was cleaned and ready to go into the oven after lunch was cleared away.

Mary McCarty sighed. Cook, clean, cook, clean, cook again. Her life was simple. One day so much like another.

Four

Sheriff Sam Long hauled his hefty bulk out of bed, awakened by the smell of coffee perking.

Bless those girls. Up every morning at 6:00 to fix breakfast.

The lawman raised his arms over his head, stretching the kinks out of his six-foot-four frame. He splashed his face with cold water from the tap, drying quickly on the hand towel. He hung it on the rack, still thinking of his daughters, thankful they were growing up to be good Christian young ladies.

Taking care of the house and laundry like they were grown. And not using any of this as an excuse to neglect their school work. Straight A students, both of them.

Anna Mae, the older of the two, had earned herself a spot on the girls' basketball team, even though she was only five-feet-two. *She's got stamina and backbone. Full of love and caring, too. One day, she's going to be a beautiful woman.*

Sam daubed shaving soap on his face and sharpened his straight razor. *Johnnie Ruth's coming along, too. Still a child.*

Not nearly so serious as Anna Mae. Full of fun and teasing. A joy to have around. I know both of them miss their mother.

Buttoning the vest that sported his badge, Sam walked into the kitchen where Anna was setting a platter of scrambled eggs on the table next to a pan of hot biscuits. Johnnie stood at the stove forking fried fatback out of the skillet.

"Smells good." Sam inhaled deeply. "Who made the biscuits?"

"We're not telling," the girls replied, almost in unison and laughed. "You'll have to guess," Johnnie said.

"I'd never be able to reckon that one out. You're both good cooks, just like your mama."

* * *

Samuel Calvin Long married Louisa Elizabeth Rodgers in Morristown, Tennessee, when they were in their teens. She was pretty, small boned with delicate features. So good-looking in fact, her papa, Ben, thought she could do better than Leeper Long's boy. "The storekeeper has a son," Ben Rodgers said more than once. "Why not him?"

Louisa's mama wrung her hands and cried because they were so young. Louisa's brothers offered to throw Sam off the place. With the members of the Rodgers family, Sam Long was about as popular as a tick.

But Louisa loved him. And he loved her. He vowed to take care of her and promised that their life would never be boring. So they married and in no time at all, Louisa was pregnant. She bore healthy children easily. Each year their family grew.

Eventually Sam's business opportunities brought them to Oklahoma. They settled on a farm in the community of Shady Dale, in northern Love County. The Long family – Sam, Louisa and their ten children – were close-knit and loving.

While the two youngest, Anna Mae and Johnnie Ruth, were still in grade school, Louisa began having 'female problems.' Doctors in Ardmore, the nearest town with a hospital, diagnosed uterine cancer. Sam and Louisa faced the bleak future together just as they had faced everything since they were youngsters back in Tennessee.

"Louisa, you're going to have to get well. I can't get along without you."

"Oh, Sam. You'll do fine. The children are almost grown."

"I'm not talking about the kids."

Louisa went on like she hadn't heard. "Gustie and her fella Carl are all set to get married next summer. Sammy wants to work for the Santa Fe soon as he's out of school. Then there'll be just Anna and Johnnie at home. It'll be like having no kids at all."

She laid her frail hand in his palm. "You're wanting to run for county sheriff next year, aren't you?"

"I been thinking about it."

"You can still do that. We'll move to Marietta. It's a nice town."

". . . and an apartment on the premises."

Louisa raised her eyebrows. "On the premises? You mean in the jail?"

"Now, Louisa, just like you always say, it'll be fine."

So Sam took on the job of sheriff in January, 1924. He knew the risks involved in keeping the law in a border county. Rivers and hills provided hiding places for outlaws on the lam. Prohibition kept people thirsty and bootlegging ran rampant. Stills cropped up in every stand of trees.

One rainy night in the wee hours of the morning, the phone rang, waking the Sheriff and his wife out of a sound sleep.

"Is this the sheriff? Can you come out to Doc Worthen's place? There's been a shooting and the doc's hurt bad."

Sam shook his head to clear it. "Doc Worthen shot? The hell you say! Is he dead?" The local dentist was a level-headed man who had never stirred up hot feelings so far as Sam knew. Why would anyone shoot him?

"I think he's still alive."

"Who's this calling?"

Click.

As he pulled on his pants and boots, Sam relayed the message to Louisa.

"You're not going, are you?"

"Of course. What do you expect me to do?"

"Sam, please don't go. At least don't go alone. I've never asked you to shirk your duty and I'm not doing that now. I just want you to be safe. Call someone to go with you."

Sam took her face in his hands. "Mama ... Louisa. You know I have to do this. It's my job."

Tears streamed as she put her hands over his. He kissed her softly on the lips and said, "Tell you what. You call Buddy Weaver and wake him up. Tell him I've headed out to Doc's place and to meet me there."

Which Louisa did. Sam's part-time deputy high-tailed it out Dry Creek Bed Road to Doc Worthen's acreage. The sheriff's wife had left the distinct impression that if Buddy didn't go, she would. When he got there Sam had two suspects on the ground, hands cuffed behind their backs. All that was left for the deputy to do was load them up and haul them to jail for arraignment in Judge Harper's court the next morning. Dr. Worthen's injury turned out to be a wound to his left shoulder. A little lower and it could have been fatal, but Doc Autry dug out the bullet and in a couple of weeks, Worthen was back pulling teeth.

Although Louisa fought courageously, there was little treatment available. For four years she battled the disease that ravaged her body. She died February 11, 1926. She was 43 years old.

Her life was short but, as Sam promised, never boring.

* * *

Sam swigged down the last of his coffee and pushed away from the table.

"Dee-licious, girls. As usual." He stood. "I got to go to the courthouse and file some papers this morning. I'll see you at noon."

Five

Mattie Lou Hudson hardly had time to think of Wendell Allen and their teasing banter after the door shut behind him. Putting down her hurt feelings from the scolding she'd received from Sarah Eastham, Mattie started breakfast as quickly as she could. She tied on her apron and moved around the kitchen efficiently. She poured boiling water in the Drip-o-later, stepped back and watched the brown liquid fall into the coffee pot below. *Newfangled geegaw. Soon as something different comes out* she *has to have it.*

Mattie had heard housewives — even Mrs. Eastham's friends — argue that one cannot get a good cup of coffee pouring the water over the grounds only once, rather than percolating or boiling it for several minutes. But Sarah was intrigued by the unique invention and loved being the first housewife in town to own the latest kitchen object.

Mattie Lou brought the hot biscuits, grits, scrambled

eggs and bacon into the dining room and set them on the sideboard. *Who eats breakfast in the dining room? The kitchen is good enough for most people.*

Sarah Eastham entered and stood for a moment glaring at Mattie Lou. "Mr. Eastham is waiting for his breakfast, if you *please.*" Mattie scurried through the swinging door to the kitchen and returned with a pitcher of milk just as Sarah was saying to her husband, "… late again today." Mattie retreated before the door stopped moving.

"Mmmm," Frank responded, his eyes scanning a story in the Oklahoma City newspaper about a bank robbery in Madill. Ever the banker, he always studied these incidents with care, trying to see where the bank personnel might have erred.

Fifteen copies of the *Daily Oklahoman* were delivered each morning to Marietta at the premium price of five cents a copy. Of those, ten were left for resale at Kelley's Drug Emporium. Individual papers were delivered to the *Marietta Monitor* newspaper office and to the Downtown Café, for the benefit of their breakfast customers. Issues also went to the homes of Frank Eastham, Aaron McCarty, and Sheriff Sam Long. If Sarah treated herself to the latest fad in household goods, then Frank did likewise to keep abreast of the daily news.

"I might just have to let her go. I'm sure there are other young girls looking for honest work. It shouldn't be hard to replace her." Sarah filled plates with the steaming food, put one in front of Frank and the other in her own place. She sat and shook out her napkin.

Though Frank seemed to be a world away, he picked up on his wife's remarks. "Now, now, Sarah. Being a few minutes late isn't the end of the world. What are you getting so worked up about?"

"I'm sure she was lollygagging out in the yard with that Wendell Allen. Right out front for all the neighbors to see."

Frank chuckled. "When did you begin to care what the neighbors think? It's for them to worry about what *you* think." He laid the newspaper aside and spooned gravy onto his biscuits.

"Oh, Frank, that's not so. You know I don't have an uncharitable bone in my body."

Frank took a sip of coffee. "What's for supper tonight?"

"Pot roast. Oh, I just remembered. Do you mind if I use the car today? I have some errands to run — and garden club of course."

"Fine. I can eat lunch at the drugstore."

"Will you want me to drive you to the bank?" She looked down at the silk lounging pajamas and house slippers she wore.

"No, dear. I can walk. It's a little brisk out today, but I'll wear my heavy coat."

"You know, some families nowadays find it handy to have two cars."

"Now don't start that. One car is sufficient for two people. I'll not even discuss it." He wiped his mouth with the linen napkin. "Next you'll want someone to drive it for you."

"W-e-l-l-l . . ."

"Enough," he said, rising. He didn't want to be reminded this morning that he had a great deal of money. He was still stinging from the accusations hurled at him last night by Sam Long, the only person in Marietta bold enough to stand up to Frank Eastham.

It had all come about at the County Commissioners' meeting when, in the course of business, there was discussion of a raise for the sheriff. The talk was fairly positive and it looked like the vote might carry, until Frank took the floor.

"I appreciate that Mr. Long is a widower with two daughters to raise, but that's not the fault nor the responsibility of this Board. There is very little crime in Marietta or in the rest of Love County for that matter — hardly enough to keep a lawman busy. And besides, we furnish the sheriff with a nice apartment — rent-free. It's my opinion that his yearly salary of $1000, plus housing, is quite adequate."

Sam Long pulled himself upright in his chair. "Just a minute, Frank." He wagged a beefy finger in the direction of the banker. "When I came here four years ago, no one could say there wasn't enough crime to keep me busy. The hills were full of stills — I broke up brawls every evening. Come Saturday night, some woman in town got beat by her drunken husband. Sure there's not much ruckus now, but why do you suppose that is?"

"Now, Sam . . ."

"And as for the nice apartment you furnish for me and the girls, let me point out that if we didn't live there, the county would be out the money to hire a jailer."

In the end, none of the Commissioners had the courage to vote 'yes' when Frank Eastham voted 'no.' There would be no raise in salary for Sheriff Long this year. Then, as the meeting broke up, Sam hit a real sore spot when he made a remark accusing Frank Eastham of being uncaring.

"You've got so much you don't have any idea what it's like for most people in this county," the burly sheriff had said. "Or maybe you know, but you don't care." He paused. "You'd do well to read your Bible about the rich man and Lazarus. Might be one day you'll be begging someone to dip his finger in the water and cool your tongue."

Sam had no right to talk to Frank that way. The lawman was angry and letting his mouth lead his brain.

Frank was not born rich. His dad was a carpenter who prospered during the years when Marietta was growing.

New houses and businesses were going up all over town. But as old Mr. Eastham aged, work slowed down. A few years before, a local resident passed away and his wife put their place up for sale, three acres with a house and a shop. Frank's brother James suggested they buy it for their parents. Sarah argued that old Mr. and Mrs. Eastham probably didn't want to move — would be happier to stay where they had been for so many years.

James' wife Edna broke the impasse. She wondered aloud what people would think if they knew that the father of the most prominent couple in town drew a county pension, while his children lived in nice houses. With that, Sarah promptly agreed to Frank and James buying the small acreage for their parents.

His brother often hinted that Frank should contribute more to their parents' living expenses — but James didn't understand how much money it took to keep Sarah happy.

The banker looked across the table at his comely wife and felt a rush of affection. *How did I ever attract such a beauty? How can I be expected to deny her anything?*

He stuck the folded newspaper under his arm and strode around the end of the table to stand beside her. She turned her cheek up for his kiss.

"I'll see you at supper," he said. "Have a good day, my love."

Six

Jake Wooley pushed open the door of the farmhouse he'd lived in most of his life. He stomped inside, bringing a cold gust of wind with him. He shrugged out of his coat, hung it on the peg and tossed his cap in the same general direction.

His wife, Cora, standing at the stove, looked over her shoulder at him. "You done milking already?"

"Don't take long to squeeze out what little Muley's got to give. She'll be plumb dry by next week." He set the milk bucket on the shelf by the dry sink.

Cora's mouth tightened into a straight line as she set the crock in the sink and strained the less-than-half gallon of milk through a clean cheese cloth. Finished, she whirled to face Jake. "What are you going to do?"

"About what?"

"About everything. We got no money. Running out of food. Cellar's near empty. Kids is barefoot. Your Mama's feeling poorly. Probably getting sick from this drafty house. We got more leaks in the roof than we got pots to put under them." She stood, hands on hips, feet spread. "What are you going to do about taking care of your family?"

"Cain't I walk in the door without hearing you belly-ache? Just shut your mouth before I shut it for you." He yanked out a chair and sat at the table. "Get me my breakfast."

Cora poured a mug of coffee from the pot on the stove and set it in front of him. Over the years she had mastered the art of setting a cup down firmly enough to give the "I ain't your maid" message, but not hard enough to spill the coffee. She placed a steaming bowl of mush and a pitcher of sorghum on the cracked oilcloth that covered the table.

Jake looked at his breakfast with distaste but dug in hungrily without a word. He glanced at Cora. Just a glance, though. Nothing like the way he used to look at her.

Look at what ten years can do to a woman. She don't care nothin about takin care of herself, or looking pretty for her man. Some women can have a house full of kids and still take care of theirself. But not Cora. Why cain't she be more like Mama?

Jake's mama, Rose Wooley, was a genteel and attractive woman who married for love, not money. First thing of a morning, she washed her face and brushed her hair into a tight bun, not a strand out of place. She had only two dresses, but she was always clean, went to church on Sundays and had a sweet word for everyone. Helped out the family by sewing for the ladies in town. *Whatever I do to make things better around here, it'll be for Mama. Not for Cora. Frumpy old grouch.*

Jake finished off his bowl of mush and molasses and wiped his mouth on his sleeve. He pulled on his coat and cap, grabbed his coffee and headed out the back door.

Buttoning his coat against he morning chill, he walked past the barn about 100 yards down the cow path to a stand of trees. The grass still icy from last night's frost crunched under his boots. He slipped between the trees to a small opening where a 1925 Model T stood just out of sight of the house.

Jake scraped the heel of his boot in the moist dirt, gathered a handful and rubbed it on the car's license plate. When it didn't stick, he poured half of his coffee on the ground, scooped up a ball of mud. He smeared it across the tin, covering the numbers.

"Hey Jake, you out here?" Jake heard his brother Cecil call from the edge of the timberline.

"I'm in here."

"What are you doing, anyway?"

Jake stepped back from the car, wiping his hands on his jacket. "Looky there. Nobody would guess this car come from Texas."

Last night they'd crossed the Red River into Texas to visit their cousin Otis in Gainesville. They told Otis a big story about their Mama wanting to visit her sister in Oklahoma City and asked if they could borrow his car, promising to have it back in two days. They left their truck at Otis' to pick up later.

Cecil looked at the car and shook his head. "Jake, you act like we do this ever day. Have you even thought about the mess we'd be in if we get caught?"

"That ain't gonna happen, big brother."

"Everybody knows us. They'll be after us before we clear town."

"They won't know us. Not with bandanas covering our faces. All they'll see is my Colt and your '38. Now, 'bout noon time we're going into town. We're going to get what we got coming to us. Then we'll high-tail it out of Love County in a car that ain't nobody seen before."

"And if we're followed?"

"Ain't nobody knows these back roads like you and me. How they gonna keep up with us? That cave back of Miller's farm is big enough to hide this car, and I done left some supplies for us, just in case we have to hole up for a few days."

"You got it all figured out, don't you."

"I sure do. You just listen to me and do what I say and you'll be fine."

Cecil turned back toward the house, muttering. "Yeah. Sure. I'll be glad when this day is over."

Seven

Sam Long pulled on his long woolen overcoat and driving gloves. Donning his white Stetson, he stepped out the door into the January sunshine. He enjoyed the walk he took each morning around the square to the courthouse.

The Love County courthouse was built in 1910 on Main Street, using a city block between NW 3rd and NW 4th Streets. The octagonal structure with four large columns at each entrance was the first courthouse built after statehood.

On the southeast corner of the property stood a free-standing building that housed the jail on the second floor. The downstairs consisted of an office for the Sheriff, an interrogation room, and a small two-bedroom apartment, where Sam and his family lived.

Marietta was an old town, declared the county seat of Love County when Indian Territory became the state of Oklahoma in 1907. One story stated that the first postmaster named the town for his wife, Mary, and his sister, Etta.

Love County, bordered on the south by Texas and the Red River, was considered a safe haven for outlaws trying to escape the famed Texas Rangers. That is, until Sam Long became sheriff.

While living in Tennessee, Sam and Louisa Long heard of the opportunities in Oklahoma, and the year after statehood they loaded their five children, George, Arthur, Claude, Walt, and Katie Minerva, on a passenger train and moved to the brand new state. They settled in the Shady Dale community where Sam owned and operated a large steam powered threshing machine, contracting with the wheat farmers in the area. The older boys helped in the threshing business. During the next six years, five more children, Clarence, Augusta, Sammy, Anna Mae and Johnnie Ruth, were born to the couple.

As the Long sons reached maturity they left home to seek fortune or adventure with the Santa Fe railroad or the U.S. Army. The oldest daughter, Katie Minerva, fell in love with a local boy and married.

Sam became interested in law enforcement. He saw an opportunity to work at a job that was not dependent on the weather. He was tired of managing work crews. His marksmanship skills, perfected while hunting in the Tennessee hills, were outstanding. Sam was known as an honest man who couldn't be bribed. When election year rolled around, he was voted County Commissioner of Washington Township, but he was really interested in the post of County Sheriff.

In 1923 he ran for sheriff and, based on his record in Washington Township, he won by an overwhelming majority. He took office the next January, the first sheriff of Love County to be elected to a four-year term.

The next years saw Marietta prosper and grow to 1,500 souls under the leadership of Mayor Aaron McCarty and the security of honest law enforcement. The Santa Fe Railroad served the town with both passenger and freight trains. There were seven cotton gins, a sawmill, three lumber yards and a movie house recently remodeled to allow accompanying sound with the Movietone News.

Sam turned the corner on the south side of the square and waved to Emory Carroll, one of the 'spit and whittle' crowd, on his way to the Downtown Café.

"Mornin' Sam. You comin in for coffee?"

"Not right now. Just had my breakfast. Maybe later."

In January 1928, the United States was near the end of the Jazz Age. Calvin Coolidge was President. Prohibition had been the law for nine years. Women had voted in the last two elections, some even taking advantage of the secret ballot to cast their vote the way they chose, rather than how their husbands directed. The 19th Amendment had given women a sense of freedom not felt before. According to the men who gathered at the

Downtown Cafe every morning to drink coffee and discuss the world's problems, some females had gotten downright uppity with their newly-won rights.

Parents all across the country felt concerns about the youth. Big city newspapers claimed prohibition — openly defied by society — was causing disrespect for all law. Preachers warned that moral standards were disappearing. Girls cropped their hair into boyish bobs. They wore short flimsy skirts that showed a shocking amount of leg when they danced.

But Marietta was far removed from most of this. Church gatherings and high school sports influenced the social life of the town. Parents kept tight control on their children, the movies they watched, music they played and parties they attended. Appropriate Sunday afternoon entertainment was a drive into the country, possibly south to Red River or north to Turner Falls, arriving home early enough for Sunday evening church services.

Though the United States as a whole was experiencing economic growth, times were still hard for the local rural folks who lived off the land. Farmers in Oklahoma shipped their crops and goods to distributors up north, but many still barely eked out a living from their land. During months of drought, they were forced to borrow money on next year's crops, then had to struggle to repay the bank loans.

Sam hated it when he was called upon to serve

foreclosure papers. It was his duty and he did it — but he didn't have to like it.

In anticipation of running for sheriff, Sam became involved in the State Peace Officers Association, attending camps where the rudiments of law enforcement were taught. In a short time, his skill with handguns was well known. He regularly brought home honors from the shooting competitions. As soon as he was elected, Sam assembled a worthy group of deputies. Jim Randolph, Under Sheriff, could be counted on to take the helm if needed. Buddy Weaver, Barney Wallace and John Wester were all loyal and dependable, even if lacking in real experience.

One day, shortly after Sam was sworn in, he and Barney drove over to Madill to pick up a prisoner. When the jailer brought the con out of the cell, Sam said to the man, "Turn around and put your hands up."

"What are you doing, Sam?" Barney asked.

"I'm fixing to search this man."

"Search him? What for? He's been in a jail cell. What do you expect to find?"

"You never know." Sam expertly ran his hands over the man's body and extracted a knife from inside the prisoner's sock. He turned and handed it to Barney.

"Always search 'em, Son," Sam said. "Always search 'em."

Eight

Anna slipped the silk stocking over her foot and smoothed it gently up her leg, fastening the garter around her thigh. She pulled on her favorite dress, red wool flannel with pleated skirt falling to just below her knee. Although she didn't own much jewelry and seldom wore it to school, today she hooked her mother's locket around her neck. *Mama is on my mind a lot today.* She gazed in the mirror and touched the locket, remembering...

* * *

It was winter, 1926. Anna entered the room quietly, leaned over the bed and kissed Louisa's cheek. The skin felt dry and papery to the young girl's lips.

"How are you feeling today, Mama?"

"Just tolerable."

Anna fluffed the pillow her papa had slept on the night before and straightened the quilts. The fourteen-year-old helped Louisa to a sitting position, putting two pillows behind her back and one under her knees.

"I'll be back with your coffee in a minute. Is there anything you want right now?"

"Would you raise the window shade?"

"Sure, Mama." Immediately the sun streamed in, filling the sick room with light. "Oh my!" the young girl said, "The sun's bright this morning."

"Ahh. It feels good — warm. Yesterday there was a squirrel playing around out there. I want to see what he's up to."

Anna peered out the window. "Really? Where?"

"In the old pecan tree yonder. I reckon he's got his winter food hidden there." Louisa rested against the pillows, closed her eyes and sighed.

Anna smiled. *Such a little thing as a squirrel carrying on in the sunshine makes her feel better.* She picked her papa's shirt off the chair, gathered a few pieces of wash from around the room and started for the door.

"Anna Mae. Wait . . ."

She hurried back to the bedside. "Yes?"

"Sit here by me a minute."

Anna lowered herself onto the patchwork beside her mama's thin body.

"I'm sorry, Anna . . ."

"For what, Mama?"

"You're too young to have to be a nurse maid."

"No, Mama . . ."

"You should be out skipping rope and playing jacks — not carrying slop jars and bathing a sick woman."

"Mama, do you think I care? Do you think I'd want anyone else to take care of you?"

"Anna Mae, when I'm gone . . ."

"Don't, Mama . . ."

"You take my locket. Johnnie Ruth can have the brooch."

"Ohhh, Mama. Thank you."

"And there's something else. You need to listen . . ."

Anna grew quiet, a tear making its way down her face. Louisa drew a shallow breath.

"I know after I'm gone there'll be lots to tend to, taking care of a house and your papa."

"Yes, ma'am."

"You teach Johnnie Ruth to help you. She's the baby and maybe we've been easy on her. But she can already cook some and when the time comes she can learn to help you do for your Papa."

"Yes, ma'am."

"Hear me, Anna Mae. What I'm saying is this: Don't you quit school."

"Oh."

"I mean it. You love school. You're smart — always making good marks. You and Johnnie Ruth too. You both stay in school. You can manage. I'll tell Papa you need to stay in school."

"All right, Mama." Anna swallowed and spoke through her grief. She released the wad of clothes, took her mother's hand and lay her head on the pillow inches from the pale one.

"I love you, Mama."

"I love you, too, Anna Mae. You're a good girl."

* * *

Anna regarded herself again in the mirror. She wiped the moisture from her eyes with the tips of her fingers. Touching her lips and then the locket, she whispered, "Love you *always*, Mama."

Nine

Sam Long and Virgil Wooley might have been friends, if Sam hadn't been sheriff and Virgil hadn't been a bootlegger.

Most folks in Love County thought highly of their sheriff. Law abiding citizens found comfort in the fact that Sam kept no office hours — he was on call 24 hours a day. Elsie McNutt's parents didn't hesitate at calling the lawman at midnight one Friday night when Elsie was two hours late coming home from the basketball game. Sam dutifully drove all the back roads and lovers' lanes. The young girl was found safe and sound, so to speak, in the back seat of Monte Taylor's Model A. When Old Man Gaines discovered one of his milk cows missing at 4:30 one morning, he roused Sam out of bed. Parents felt secure in the knowledge that the sheriff saw to it that there was not an abundance of bathtub gin in the county for their adolescents to sample.

Of course, several people in Love County chose to

make a living by producing liquor. Sam believed that in addition to being dangerous for the youngsters, whiskey was illegal. He figured it wasn't up to him to judge what a farmer chose to do with the corn he raised. Nor did it matter how Sam himself might feel about taking a drink now and then. When all was said and done, it was Sam's duty to uphold the law, and that's what he was bound to do.

Virgil Wooley had a poor farm out between Marietta and Thackerville. He and his two sons struggled to support their family with slim crops from useless fields that needed to lie fallow for at least a year. What would they do if they went a year without planting? The answer was easy. They would go hungry. Maybe starve.

Virgil and his sons devised a plan. They would let some of the fields rest and plant the others in corn. All they needed was a still, wooden barrels and fruit jars. Things moved along fairly well. The Wooleys had hopes this enterprise would see them through the winter. Then Sam Long came poking around. Said he'd kept hearing reports that someone nearby was selling corn whiskey. He wanted to know what Virgil knew about it.

Sam found the still and all the makings in the woods behind the Wooleys' house. He took the backside of an axe to the barrels and jars, yanked out the copper tubing and pushed the still into the creek. He arrested Virgil and hauled him before the county judge.

"Virgil Wooley, you're charged with making illegal spirits. How do you plead?" Judge Harper stared down at the beleaguered farmer through his Ben Franklin spectacles.

"Not guilty."

"Sheriff Long, are you bringing charges against this man?"

"Yes, Judge. I found a working distillery, 10 bushels of corn chops, bags of sugar and all the equipment for making liquor. It was in the woods — fifty yards from Mr. Wooley's back door."

Virgil spoke up. "It weren't mine, Judge. Musta been trespassers put it there. I don't know nothing about a still. They musta stole my corn."

Judge Harper nodded solemnly. "Did Sheriff Long have a warrant to search your farm?"

"He had some kinda paper. I don't read too good." Virgil drew himself up, his sun-weathered face turning crimson. "You know, Judge, the sheriff come on my land waving a paper. I don't know what it said. He just come drivin up into the yard, scarin the kids and the chickens. He didn't have no right to get into my business and he sure didn't have no right to pour out my mash!"

Since Virgil hung himself right there in court, the judge had no choice but impose the sentence, "Thirty dollars or fourteen days." Virgil, short of money, was obliged to spend a fortnight in the Love County jail.

The inmates of the local clink got two meals a day, as was usual in most lockups. The cells were small as dungeons, but the food was better than most inhabitants ever tasted. In the small apartment, Johnnie Ruth and Anna Mae turned out plenty of mouth-watering food. They were excellent cooks, having learned during the years Sam owned and operated the threshing machine. It was the girls' duty to cook every day for the threshing crew, a bawdy bunch who could eat their weight in biscuits and gravy and didn't mind telling a sensitive young girl if the biscuits were hard or the gravy lumpy. Love County prisoners never complained.

In addition to relishing the good jail food, Virgil also found he enjoyed the nightly domino games with Sam Long and anyone else who might be a temporary guest of the county. The two men were evenly matched as far as skill, but Sam was more disciplined. The sheriff never gave away his hand. Not even by a twitch of the eyebrow.

Virgil left at the end of his two weeks' stay with no hard feelings toward the sheriff. He even shook Sam's hand, saying, "You got a job to do and so do I. We'll prolly meet again."

However, for Virgil's sons, Jake and Cecil, it was a different story. Jake was furious at Sam. It had taken the three men a month to build that operation and it was a fine one. Besides banging up the still and spilling out the fermenting mash, Sam had left the whole place strewn with busted jars and broken kegs. He had cost the Wooleys a good part of their livelihood. Cecil didn't say much as he set about putting things together so they could be back in business as soon as possible. They had promised a delivery to a speak-easy down on Red River by the end of the week. Jake stomped and fumed as he picked up broken glass and barrel staves.

"Who does that sheriff think he is? Kaiser Bill? This is the U.S. of A. We got a right to support our family." He kicked at a tangle of copper tubing. "I'll get even with Sam Long if it's the last thing I do."

Ten

Two days later, Jake Wooley was still mad. After he'd finished milking, he slammed into the barn, yanked off his cap and threw it at the remains of the still, which was nothing but a mess of metal lying on the floor.

"What's wrong with you?" Cecil looked around from the work bench where he was skinning a rabbit.

"All this here pipe is tore up. I'm gonna have to patch every piece of that still to get it back together. And half our jars is broke."

"Well, I got good news. Look here." He held up the rabbit carcass. "Shot 'im this morning. Rabbit for supper."

"Got any taters or carrots? I'll wager not."

"Don't matter. It'll taste good anyway." Cecil looked up and grinned. "Soon's I finish here, I'll give you a hand. We just need to keep at it. We'll get it fixed. Next time we'll find a better hiding place. What else can we do?"

Jake picked up his cap and slapped it against his leg a

couple of times to shake off the dust. "I been thinking. I know what we can do."

"What's that?"

"You're not going to like it."

"What?"

"If you don't want to help, I'll do it by myself."

"What?"

"Rob the bank."

"Don't talk crazy. We cain't rob no bank."

"Yes, we can. I got it all planned out." When Cecil didn't answer, Jake went on. "Look how they treated us. They got a nerve coming out here demanding payment when times is hard. Worrying Papa and making Mama cry."

Cecil continued to clean the rabbit, cutting it up and tossing the pieces in a bucket of water. When he finished, he stabbed his knife into the wooden bench and turned to his brother. His eyes grew serious.

"Okay. You're right. They're a bunch a rich folks don't care about no one but theirselves. But you're forgetting one thing. Sam Long."

"Never you mind the sheriff. He cain't be everywhere all the time. We'll wait till he's out doing his lawman stuff, out here in these woods, nosing around for moonshiners, looking to hinder hard-working people. When he's out with that axe looking to bust stuff up, that means he ain't watching things in town. And that's when we'll go take that bank for all they got."

"Jake, you need to get over your mad at the sheriff. He's the *sheriff.* He's got the law behind him."

"Who? What law? Are you afraid of Jim Randolph?"

"Yes, him. And lawmen all over the county. They all stick together — all the way to the state police."

"That don't matter. You leave him to me. I ain't forgot he's the one give us the hard times we got now. How'd he expect us to feed our families if we cain't sell a little liquor along the way. If he tries to stop us from taking back money that was took from us — well, it'll be the last time the S.O.B. gets in somebody's way."

Eleven

Sarah Eastham stood in her spacious upstairs bathroom, in front of the full-length mirror. The dressing gown slid from her shoulders and dropped to the floor. She had always been grateful for her slim figure and enjoyed gazing at it. Once, when she was a blossoming teen, her mother had caught her brazenly admiring her bare body and told her it was unladylike, disgraceful, and *sinful* to stand and stare at one's own nakedness.

As Sarah matured, she turned into a real beauty, never lacking for beaus. She chose Frank Eastham carefully. She learned early in her marriage how to use her loveliness to get what she wanted. Frank's reluctance to host dinner parties in their home was overcome with a simple promise: "When the party is over, and everyone has gone home, I'll let you watch me undress." These were the rare times when Frank saw her completely nude, and he was like putty in her hands. She knew that whenever she surprised Frank by slipping into bed wearing absolutely nothing, the next day she could ask for whatever she wanted.

She narrowed her eyes and looked critically at her image. She noticed the bit of extra flesh at the top of her legs, the slight sag of her breasts. She would be thirty-five years old on her next birthday. Near the age to need beauty treatments. *A facial every day would remove those lines from around my eyes. And a massage regularly would keep my skin and muscles firm.*

Frank saw these treatments as luxuries, Sarah considered them necessities. *If I lose my looks, how much longer will I be able to tease Frank into giving me the things I need?*

Sarah was happy there had been no children to ruin her perfect figure. Frank had hoped for a son, had talked of it often when they first married. But so far the secret Sarah's mother had passed on to her worked, and every 28 days, her visitor came round, regular as clockwork.

Originally, when Sarah started dating Frank, she chose him as a stepping-stone. But when she found no man richer than Frank to set her sights on — and realized how difficult a divorce would be — she changed her plan. If they were in a large bank — in a bigger city with a more exciting social life . . . Well, she simply must influence Frank to move up the ladder to grander things.

But, Sarah found Frank's business decisions were his alone and she was unable to sway him. He could have moved up in the world, if only he'd wanted to. He had a chance once at a bank in Ardmore. And another in Pauls

Valley. But Frank loved this one-horse town with its country folks. He liked to say he was helping them.

So, Sarah had to be content as the reigning pacesetter of Marietta social life. She organized a garden club and — with a bit more difficulty — a bridge club. She easily took over as leader of the Women's Missionary Society. A few acceptable couples made it into her circle of acquaintances who might be invited to dinner. She was careful to associate with only those of good heritage. Before statehood there had been some mixed marriages in Love County, and sometimes you couldn't tell just by looking that someone was part Indian. But Sarah was discerning. She preferred the company of whites only. She was firmly established as the most important matron in Marietta, Oklahoma.

The banker's wife slid down into the hot bath and thought of her day ahead. *Garden club this afternoon. Plan menu for bridge club on Friday. Make sure everyone in the Missionary Society has signed up to work in the rummage sale.* She took a soft cloth and slathered her body with Lux soap.

Maybe I'll write a letter to the Presiding Elder. Invite him and his wife to dinner. Tell him a few things he needs to know. This new Methodist preacher's stance on card playing was becoming a bother. Just last week, Sally Garvin backed out of the bridge luncheon at the last minute. She said the baby was sick. But, Sarah didn't believe her.

Sally's husband, Jack, was chairman of the Board of Stewards. Sarah was guessing he told Sally she couldn't attend a card party. *That's the only way the mousy thing would have the nerve to turn down an invitation from* me!

Sarah was reaching for a towel when the telephone rang. Hurrying into the bedroom, she snatched the receiver off the bedside table.

"Hello?"

"Hello, my dear. How's your morning going?"

"Oh, hello, Frank. I'm fine. A little busy. Do you need something?"

"Yes, actually, I do. I left a large envelope of papers there on my desk. I need them this afternoon. Can you possibly bring them down? Perhaps we can have lunch while you're downtown. Before you run off to your meeting."

"Oh, Frank. I have a very busy day. I really don't have time to come off downtown. Are those papers so important?"

"Yes, Sarah, they are." The light banter in his voice disappeared.

"Very well. I'll get them to you. But I can't go to lunch. Some other day, maybe."

"All right. Just please have them down here before noon." He hung up without saying goodbye.

Sarah frowned. She remembered when Frank could never hang up the phone without saying, "Love you, honey" or "I miss you, Sweetie." Just now he didn't bother to say good-bye. He spoke to her like he might speak to an employee. *Is he beginning to resist my coaxing and teasing? All the more reason to worry about how I will look ten years from now.*

She found the envelope of papers on Frank's desk. *If I take these to the bank, I won't have time to give myself a fresh manicure.* I need *a manicure. I can't go with ragged-looking nails.*

I'll send Mattie. She took the envelope of papers and headed to the kitchen.

Twelve

Anna waved at friends as she made her way to class, the heels of her pumps clicking on the hardwood floors. The bright red dress set off her blue eyes and fair skin, a legacy of her Scotch-Irish heritage. In spirit, she was mature for her age, but her round face and full lips made her look younger than her sixteen years.

I'm so glad I have English Literature first. Starts my day off right.

Students scrambled to their seats, responding with "Present" as Mr. Newton called roll.

"Good morning, class," he said, searching for the textbook on his cluttered desk. "Today we are looking at the poems of Miss Elizabeth Barrett Browning, particularly the group called *Sonnets from the Portuguese.* Miss Browning wanted to give the impression to her readers that these sonnets were written in Portuguese and that she had merely translated them. In reality, they were indeed her own compositions written in English.

"Open your texts to page 98 and read Sonnet 43 and the narrative regarding this poem. You will then either answer the questions on page 99 or write a paragraph about Miss Browning. These should be on my desk before you leave here for your next class."

Several boys moaned in protest, but only as loudly as they dared without risking retribution from Mr. Newton. Moan too loudly, and he might double the assignment. But moan not at all? No sixteen-year-old boy can be assigned to read poetry without moaning just a little.

Yet, Anna loved the assignment. While the other students were still opening their books, thumbing through the pages and fishing for pencil and paper, Anna was immersed in the words of her favorite poet, in the words of her favorite poem. *'How do I love thee? Let me count the ways.'*

She had read every sonnet, even before they were assigned, and had several favorites. Sometimes, deep in the poetry, Anna imagined herself as the fragile Elizabeth Barrett, who wrote about the depths of human love until true love at last found her.

How beautifully she describes the way she loves him ...'depth and breadth and height ... by sun and candlelight ... freely ... purely ... with the breath, smiles, tears of all my life.'

By the time Anna finished reading, tears filled her eyes. She ducked her head and unobtrusively wiped her eyes, sniffing softly as she could manage. *How would it be to love someone that much — that it consumed your whole being?*

She read the last line again. '*. . . and if God choose, I shall but love thee better after death.'* She placed the palm of her hand on the open book, savoring the words. *Is that possible? To love someone after death?*

Anna thought again of Monroe, the boy she liked so much — maybe loved. Then her mother crossed her mind. *Ohhh. What about Mama?* She touched the locket at her throat. *I still love her. And I know she's in heaven loving me. Sometimes I feel her love so strong it just wraps me up in itself and carries me along.*

Anna gazed out the window at the bright winter day. *Mama loved the sunshine. She would say, 'What a beautiful day today.'*

Mr. Newton's voice broke into her thoughts, "Miss Long, would you join us please?"

Brought back to the present, Anna grabbed her pencil and opened her notebook to write the paragraph.

"I think Miss Browning understood love better than anyone else I have ever heard describe it. Maybe this was because she was not in good health and Robert Browning's attention was such a surprise to her. The fact that her father disapproved of the romance didn't stop them at all. Nothing could dampen her love for Robert Browning. She chose her true love and was disowned by her father. This <u>must</u> have made her sad, but it was never reflected in her poetry. She was willing to give up anything for love."

What would that be like? Is there a sacrifice I would make for love? I could never give up Papa. Nor Johnnie. Her pencil poised over the paper, Anna again became lost in her own thoughts. She wrote her initials, AML, and then Monroe's, RMA, forming a cross with the common letter 'M' in the center. Startled by the bell announcing the end of class, she hastily erased the scribbled letters and finished her paragraph.

"I hope when I am an English teacher I can help my students understand the meaning of Miss Browning's wonderful poetry.

Anna Mae Long,

English Literature, First Hour,

Marietta High School,

January 28, 1928."

Thirteen

Mattie Lou Hudson gently applied silver polish to the last knife, starting at the handle and continuing with a smooth stroke to the tip. She gathered several pieces of silver and rinsed them under running water. One by one she dried the flatware with a soft cloth and returned it to the cherry wood chest.

Each time she placed the fancy box of sterling in the buffet drawer, Mattie remembered the set of Wm. A. Rogers silver plate flatware her mama had once owned. Not nearly so valuable as the Easthams' silver, but it did have its own wooden chest. It had cost her daddy a pretty penny back in the day. It about broke her mama's heart to have to sell it.

John Hudson was a wonderful daddy. Mattie and her mama, Faye, never had to worry about having presents at Christmas or new clothes for Easter. John provided well for his family on his commissions as a life insurance agent. What irony that he had never bought a policy for himself.

It was hard for Mattie when her daddy died — not just the missing of him who was so happy-go-lucky, but losing the love and security he gave. He'd come in whistling every night, swing Mama around and kiss her like it was their wedding day. Then, he would tease Mattie Lou. He made them feel the joy of being together when life was so good.

Then suddenly he was gone. Sick only a few days with the flu. Out of his head with a raging fever until the last few minutes when he opened his eyes, said "I love you" to Mattie and Faye, and asked them to pray the Lord's Prayer. Before they finished, his soul was in heaven.

Mattie hoped to finish school — and her mama wanted her to, but it was so hard to make ends meet. Faye did fancy stitching with the Singer sewing machine John had bought her when Mattie was ten. It came with an array of attachments that would do most anything a person could ask. People paid good money for the shirring and tucks Faye was able to turn out, but the need for fancy sewing wasn't steady. So she offered her ironing services to a few ladies in town. John had always bragged that Faye made his dress shirts look as good as any laundry could. Scrimping and scraping, Faye and Mattie barely got through the rest of the school year.

Then one day last summer when Sarah Eastham came to pick up her husband's shirts, she offered Mattie Lou a job. Sarah had complained that she needed help every day, not just once a week. The social demands of a bank president's wife gave her too little time to attend to the house properly. However, Mr. Eastham insisted this was an expense that was not necessary. And he assured Mrs. Eastham that this was one demand he would not indulge. And he almost meant it. Sarah had to surprise Mr. Eastham on more than one night to convince him to see things her way.

She offered to pay Mattie Lou $5.00 a week to be their fulltime maid. Mattie thought only a minute before she accepted.

Faye cried more than Mattie did the day school started in September. Mattie knew she was lucky to have a job. She accepted dropping out of school as her lot in life. But sometimes, like today, she wished she had been able to finish school with her friends.

Mattie missed Anna Mae. Now that their lives had taken different paths, they saw each other when they could manage it. But Anna was busy with school activities. Usually Mattie was bone tired when she got home from work in the evenings. Often they spent Sunday afternoons together, baking cookies or making jelly. Then it was like old times. They always parted with a hug and a promise to see each other again soon. And a vow to remain best friends forever.

Mattie's daydream was interrupted as Sarah burst through the swinging door from the dining room.

"Before you eat your lunch, I need you to run an errand downtown for me."

"Yes Ma'am."

"Take this envelope to the bank and give it to Mr. Eastham's secretary."

Mattie wiped down the cabinet top where she had been working. She took her coat off the hook by the door. Sarah continued talking.

"While you're in town, step into Kelley's and get me a paper of pins."

"Yes, Ma'am."

"And when you leave this afternoon, don't forget to take the shirts we washed yesterday. We need them ironed by Friday."

"Yes, Ma'am."

Mattie put on her coat and cap. The envelope was too large for her pocket, so she tucked it under her arm. She stopped for a moment, staring at the door still swinging from Sarah's exit.

Well, sure I'll put off my dinner and walk downtown in the freezing cold. And sure I'll haul the shirts <u>*we*</u> *washed yesterday.* Pulling a face, she yanked her hat farther down over her ears and stepped out into the winter day.

Mattie was pleased to find it was warmer than earlier that morning. Typical of Oklahoma. Dawn might break with chilling cold but the winter sunshine raised the temperature. Maybe not enough to make a seven-block walk pleasant, but at least tolerable.

I know the shirts need to be ironed, but I was hoping she'd see her way clear to take them herself and give me a ride home. So much for that idea.

It wasn't often Sarah sent Mattie on an errand. Usually she was housebound all day long catering to her mistress' whims. Once in the crisp air, she realized what a delight it was to escape the confines of those four walls. She strolled along with energy, unexpectedly enjoying the outing. Her coat was warm. She had good walking shoes. What more could she ask for right this minute?

Just as Mattie was crossing Chickasaw Street, a car whizzed by. A shiny black Model T Ford. Jake Wooley was driving. His brother, Cecil sat in the passenger seat. Neither noticed her at all.

Where'd those two Crackers get a fine car like that? Speeding through town at 25 miles an hour, at least.

Mattie immediately felt guilty at the thought. *Mama would scold me good if she heard those words. She'd say it's unchristian to call someone a cracker or to speak ill of those less fortunate.*

It's hard to think of someone less fortunate than Mama and me. But if there is, it's got to be the Wooleys.

The Wooley men were bootleggers. Everyone knew that. They ran moonshine all over Love County and down to North Texas even. Talk was all over town when Sheriff Long busted up their still last month. It's a wonder no one got shot. The Wooley boys were nothing but gangsters.

Everyone in town feels sorry for Mrs. Wooley. In church every Sunday. Always a smile. Always doing something to help others. But she's a sheep in the midst of wolves. None of the other Wooleys ever darken the door of the church. Not Old Man Virgil. Not his sons. Not even Cora. You'd think that she'd want her younguns in Sunday School, where they might hear something good for them.

Another car passed, this one full of high school kids on their way downtown. Mattie's thoughts wandered again to her former classmates. She blinked rapidly, thinking of how she missed the fun and excitement of being in school every day. The friendships, the social life — even the learning and the homework involved. She shook her head to clear it and drew a deep breath of cold air.

I think I'll go to the bank first. Get rid of this bulky envelope. Then when I stop at Kelley's, maybe I'll have myself a Coca Cola.

For a day that started not so well, Mattie was determined to do something that would lift her spirits and make this Tuesday turn out fine.

Fourteen

Marietta High School, home of the Indians, occupied the top floor of a two-story building that sat on a spacious lawn eight blocks from downtown. The younger classes met on the ground floor.

Basketball was the primary sport in the smaller school districts in Oklahoma. Any campus large enough to have five boys formed a basketball team. The principal or any male teacher with working knowledge of the game was designated coach. Poor districts without funds for a gym scheduled their games in the nearest field house that could accommodate them. Fans packed the bleachers every time their home team played, and a significant number traveled around the county supporting the players. Marietta, the largest town in Love County, had a first rate gym paid for with a millage voted five years ago. Both the boys' and girls' basketball teams were winners.

The Booster Club was proud of the Marietta Indians' basketball standings. The boys had gone to the state playoffs the last two years. Business men in town had placed a trophy case in the center of the upstairs hall with the expectation that a prize would be added each year.

Olin McCarty wasn't just his parents' pride and joy. He was Marietta's biggest star. Big Man on Campus. Captain of the basketball team. Everyone in town knew Olin McCarty. He was the reason the Booster's trophy case wasn't empty. His jump shots that never missed and his cool-as-a-cucumber free throws were going to win him a college scholarship for sure.

Olin walked down the hall that Tuesday morning to calls of "Attaboy, Olin," "Great game last night," "And how!" The Indians had beaten neighboring Thackerville by two points in overtime. Olin McCarty had scored the winning goal from mid-court — a split-second before the final buzzer.

In his morning classes, Olin turned in his book report on *Moby Dick*. He scored 100 per cent on a pop test in Algebra. He spent study hall in the library, researching his term paper. His thesis: 'Why Germany Will Never Again be a Threat to America.'

Olin's last class before lunch was English Literature. He slid into his desk and pulled the day's assignment out of his notebook: Write an original poem, any form, that shows strong emotion.

Earlier in the semester, Olin had been taken by the study of the poem, *In Flanders Fields,* by John McCrae. He loved the idea of being heroic in battle, of fighting for something grand, something that would make a difference in the world. He regretted that he had been just a child during the Great War. Thousands of American men had lost their lives or their livelihoods by becoming soldiers. Five men from Marietta had paid the ultimate sacrifice. Others would carry wounds of war forever. Olin's poem reflected all these thoughts. He raised his hand, volunteering to be the first to read. He read with confidence:

"In Flanders Fields red poppies fly
To mark the graves of those who died
The brave soldiers who gave their all
And bravely answered their nation's call.

I was a child, I could not go
Defend our land against the foe.
I want to honor the brave and yet
What can I do? I'll not forget."

Olin found his way back to his seat, to a smattering of applause.

"A good start, Olin. Needs some work. You use the word 'brave' several times. But a good start. I like the sentiment." Mr. Newton made a mark in the grade book lying on his desk. "Who next?" He scanned the room.

"Charles Leaks."

Charles Allen Leaks, Jr. was known to everyone at MHS as 'Bobo,' a nickname given him by his little sister who was obviously trying to say 'brother.' As might be assumed from the sound of his name, Bobo was the class clown. He approached the front of the room and unfolded a rumpled piece of notebook paper. Students sat up in their seats. This promised to be good.

"I had a wooden whistle
But it wooden whistle."

A rustle went through the room as students fidgeted in their seats, sneaking looks at one another. Mr. Newton raised his eyes from his grade book. Anyone who read the dime magazines sold at Kelley's Drug Emporium knew this was *not* an original poem. But did Mr. Newton know?

"So I bought a steel whistle
But it steel wooden whistle."

Several students covered their mouths with their hands. Others hid smiles behind raised textbooks. Mr. Newton's eyes narrowed slightly as he stared in Bobo's direction.

"Then I bought a lead whistle,
But steel it wooden lead me whistle."

Someone snickered out loud. Mr. Newton stood and pinned the offender with his piercing blue eyes.

"So I bought a tin whistle.

Now I tin whistle."

The room exploded in laughter. Mr. Newton grabbed his pointer — a yardstick from McCarty's Hardware — and whacked the top of his desk.

"Quiet!" The racket was silenced in mid-guffaw. "Now," he said. "Since you find this little verse so jolly, you will all spend the rest of the period writing a humorous poem. In rhyme. Iambic pentameter. At least twelve lines."

Bobo scrambled back to his seat, and everyone in the room scrounged in their desks for pencil and paper.

Mr. Newton continued, "These poems will be graded. And if I do not *laugh out loud* when I read your verse, your grade will reflect that. Now get busy. And I'd better not hear so much as a sigh."

Fifteen

At noon, both schools let out for the children to go home for lunch. Those who lived outside town took their lard buckets to the gymnasium to eat the biscuits and sorghum and fried salt pork they had brought. If a piece of chalk could be found, a hop scotch diagram was drawn on the front sidewalk.

Laughing teens piled in jalopies to race to The Malt Shop for a sandwich and a glass of Coca Cola from the new fountain. Olin McCarty did not join them. He retrieved his bicycle and pedaled downtown alone to buy pencil and paper at the five-and-dime. Olin also had plans to visit Kelley's Drug Emporium while he was in town. Josephine Kelley, a senior at Marietta High School, worked behind the counter of her father's store during her lunch break.

Olin and Josie had been in school together since the first grade, in the same Sunday School classes since Cradle Roll. She had never been anything special. Until

September.

Josie spent the month of August with her aunt in Purcell. She came back different. The light brown hair that had hung to her waist ever since Olin could remember now fell around her shoulders in a long bob. She wore the faintest bit of pink color on her lips and cheeks. The pleated jumpers and matching waists had been changed for soft wool skirts and gauzy midi-blouses. When she walked into the senior home room the first day of school, every boy took notice.

Olin pedaled furiously. The sooner he got to town the longer he could hang around Kelley's. If he was lucky, he might catch Josie's eye, might give her a wink. If his knees didn't fail him first.

He reached the corner of 4th and Main Street and walked, pushing his bike, past the Love County National Bank. He glanced through the window and stopped in his tracks. The scene in the lobby of the bank looked strange. The man standing with Mr. Eastham had his hat pulled down almost to his eyebrows. A bandana around his neck covered his mouth and chin. As Olin watched, the man withdrew his fist from his pocket. In it, he held a gun that he waved in Mr. Eastham's face.

Olin's eyes locked with those of the teller in the cage. The man's eyes, desperate with fear, widened as he indicated his head slightly toward the stranger and the bank president. The message was clear: *Get help!*

Olin ran next door to Kelley's Drug Emporium.

"Mr. Kelley, can I use your telephone?"

"Now, just calm down, boy. What do you need the phone for?"

"Something strange is going on at the bank. I want to call the law."

"Well, go on, then."

Olin tore to the back of the building where the pharmacist had his shop.

"Number, please."

"I need to talk to Sheriff Long."

"What's your business with the sheriff?"

Inez Jenkinson had been operator of the telephone exchange for ten years. When her husband died of a heart attack, she needed employment. Too proud to take in ironing, she turned to her Uncle William who owned the local telephone company. She prided herself that she had saved a lot of folks unnecessary calls by questioning the callers in advance. It was a rare patient indeed who talked to Dr. Autry without first describing the malady to Mrs. Jenkinson.

"This is Olin McCarty, Mrs. Jenkinson. I need to talk to Sheriff Long. It looks like somebody's robbing the bank!"

"What makes you think that?"

"I can see the man through the window. Please, Mrs. Jenkinson."

"Very well, I will notify the sheriff. You can go on about your business." She was not about to let an over-excited young boy bother Mr. Long while he ate his lunch.

Olin flew out the front door of Kelley's and biked two blocks down West Main to his dad's hardware store. He ran down the side aisle and grabbed a shotgun off the rack. His hand searched below the counter for ammunition.

"Hey, Olin. What are you doing?" Floyd Hyde came from behind the tool counter where he had been stocking merchandise. He was a veteran of the Great War, old beyond his years. He was a husband with the responsibility of a wife and young child. Olin was the boss's son. But, he was still just a kid.

"I'm getting me a gun," Olin said, sticking extra shells in his jacket pocket. "Somebody's robbing the bank."

"No, now." Carefully taking hold of the gun stock, Floyd wrested it away from the boy. "Your dad's gone to eat. You get on home now. Tell your Papa whatever's bothering you."

"But I tell you, there's bank robbers . . ."

"If something's happening at the bank, that's the law's business. Let him take care of it. I'm not gonna let you get yourself killed."

Besides being ten years older, Floyd spoke with the authority of a man who knew he was in charge. Olin quickly decided there was no time to argue. He ran from the hardware store, jumped on his bicycle and headed toward home.

Sixteen

She would never admit it, but it was at Louisa Long's funeral that Inez Jenkinson first took notice of Sheriff Long, in the sense that a woman notices a man. She saw him being stoic in his grief. A strong support for his girls. She thought about how empty he must feel. She also noticed what a fine looking man he was — and set her cap for him. Before Louisa was in the ground, Inez made up her mind.

After all, she had been a widow for over ten years. She was ready to find herself another man. And surely Sam would soon need a wife to help see after his girls.

Every week or so, beginning shortly after the funeral, Inez carried a sample of her cooking over to the Long household — fried chicken, custard pie, or her special chocolate layer cake. She was eager to let Sam see how handy she was in the kitchen. Let the girls see it, too. Maybe they would be happy to have another woman in the house. Take some of the load off of them.

It became Inez's habit each Sunday morning to walk to the pew where the Longs sat. Saying good morning to Sam and the girls, she would engage one of them in animated conversation until Brother Fleming announced the first hymn. Then she would say, "Oh my, the service is starting," and quickly drop down onto their pew. She had become expert at her timing.

Lately, Sam had taken to sitting with Anna on one side and Johnnie on the other, but that didn't deter Inez. There beside one of the girls in the second pew, pulpit side, she felt the whole congregation could see what a nice-looking family they would make.

As a year passed and neared two, Inez realized that Sam was not the sort to choose a mate hastily. He was devoted to Anna and Johnnie. Inez had no children of her own, so she thought perhaps she needed to demonstrate that given the chance she could be a good mother to girls in their teens.

Nice young girls. Mannerly enough. But they could use a woman's hand. Sam doesn't pay enough attention to what the girls wear. Bobbed hair and rolled down hose! They need a woman's hand so that they become young ladies, not tomboys. I'll just have to tread easily. Be tactful.

Seeing Sam downtown one afternoon, she seized the opportunity.

"Sheriff Long — ah, Sam — I saw Anna's picture in

the Monitor with the girls' basketball team. I was surprised."

"Were you really? I'm not surprised. She's little, but she's quick."

"Yes, but do you think all that running around like a boy is good for a young girl?"

"They don't run like the boys. They only play on half the court. It don't hurt her. Or Johnnie either. She's coming right along behind Anna."

"But — how can I say this — a girl's — *body parts* are delicate. I don't know what the school board was thinking to allow a girl's sport in the school."

Sam drew a deep breath, narrowed his eyes. "Thank you for your advice, Miss Inez, but I think my girls are just fine."

"Well, maybe so. But, you know, some young girls need help learning to become young women."

"Good day to you, Miss Inez."

"Oh, all right. Good day," she said to his retreating back.

You might walk away from me now, Sheriff Long, but you'll come around. When you see what I can do for you and your girls, you'll come around.

Seventeen

The milk run over, Wendell Allen unhitched Beulah. He gave the mare to the stable boy, who tied on her feedbag and rubbed her down. Wendell patted her on the rump, said, "See you tomorrow, old girl," and walked from the barn out into the winter day.

He liked his job at Gaines Dairy. It required him to roll out of bed before the roosters, but the pay was decent. He arrived at the dairy farm every morning while it was still dark, to help finish up whatever milking and straining was left to be done before he hitched up the mare and loaded the milk wagon. He relished riding through the streets of Marietta just as the town woke up. He could say good morning to folks and maybe bring them some news about their neighbors. About noon, after all the empty bottles were put in the sterilizer, his job at Gaines was done and the rest of the day was his to do as he pleased.

Wendell had promised his papa that this afternoon

he would go straight home and fix the mailbox post that was leaning. He couldn't figure why his mama worried so much about that mailbox. Wendell didn't know the last time they got any mail.

Once a year the mailman brought the Sears Roebuck catalog. Around Christmas an insurance company up north sent a calendar with pictures of nice scenery or famous people. In fact, even though the Allen family had never been able to afford insurance, that calendar had a lot to do with how Wendell got his name. When a baby boy arrived after four girls, Wendell's mama and papa had not thought of a proper name for their first-born son. Papa looked at the calendar to mark down the date and noticed Assistant Chief Justice Oliver Wendell Holmes staring back at him. "Such a fine boy," Papa said. "We'll just name him after a judge."

I'd best head on home. But first I need to go downtown to Kelley's for a sack of tobacco and some rolling papers.

It was a two-mile walk into town but Wendell strode along briskly, whistling *Bringing in the Sheaves*. Wendell loved church songs. Especially if he could manage it so Mattie was standing beside him, holding one page of the hymnbook while he held the other. He thought of the smell of her fresh-scrubbed skin, sunshiny curls falling to her shoulders.

A melody from the new Cokesbury Hymnal came to him and he raised his voice in a swinging rendition of

Love Lifted Me, Love Lifted Me. He imagined Mattie Lou's fair head tilted over the hymnbook. And he was no longer thinking about the love of Jesus.

When he turned the corner on the north side of the square, Wendell saw what he thought at first was a daydream. Mattie Lou Hudson was crossing the street in front of Kelley's a block away. *What's she doing downtown in the middle of the day?* He almost called to her but caught himself just in time. No nice young girl wants her name hollered clear across downtown. He trotted to catch up with her, but she turned and stepped into the bank.

Well, darn. I don't want to follow her in there where her boss works. I'll get my fixins and stand in front of Kelley's until she comes out. Then I can say 'howdy' and maybe get to talk to her a while.

Inside Kelley's Drug Emporium, Wendell spent a little extra time looking at the line of sundries Mr. Kelley had in stock. *I'd like to buy a present for Mattie Lou. But what's the proper thing to give a young lady you're not engaged to?* A flower would be nice — but it was the dead of winter. No flowers growing anywhere around and a fellow would have to go clear to Ardmore to find a hothouse florist.

Wendell looked up when Olin McCarty rushed in the front door and brushed by without so much as a 'howdy-do.' Which was a strange way for Olin to act. Wendell and Olin had been in the same class at Marietta School until Wendell quit to go to work for Mr. Gaines. Olin ran over to where the druggist was putting up a display of trusses.

"Mr. Kelley, can I use your telephone?"

"Now, just calm down, boy. What do you need the phone for?"

Wendell didn't hear Olin's answer. But Mr. Kelley's eyebrows went way up into his hairline and he pointed toward the back of the store where the telephone hung on the wall. Curiosity got the better of Wendell and he followed Olin down the aisle past shelves of water bottles and health tonics.

"This is Olin McCarty, Mrs. Jenkinson. I need to talk to Sheriff Long. Somebody's robbing the bank."

Olin listened for a minute, then said into the phone, "I can see the man through the window. *Please*, Mrs. Jenkinson."

Without hearing any more of Olin's conversation, Wendell sprinted back up the aisle and pushed through the front door. He barely heard Mr. Kelley's voice behind him, "Hey, you. Allen kid. Stop running in here!"

Wendell crossed the street and paused at the edge of the large window, hiding himself from view of anyone inside as he peeked into the bank. Sure enough, there stood Mattie Lou, her back to the teller's cage, hands raised, eyes wide.

Mattie Lou's in danger! Wendell took a deep breath, tried

to think. *The sheriff's on the way. Olin just called him. All I have to do is stall the robbers until he gets here.*

Wendell Allen took off his cap and ran his hands through his sandy hair. Setting the cap at a jaunty angle, he squared his shoulders, pulled the heavy door open and walked into the bank.

Eighteen

When school let out for lunch, Anna Mae Long walked as fast as a young lady dared, covering the few blocks from the high school to the family apartment in the jail.

Anna slipped her hand in the mailbox marked 'Sheriff Long' and pulled out the morning mail, hoping for a letter from Monroe.

She'd met the handsome musician last June while spending the summer with her older sister, Augusta. Gustie and her husband, Carl Locke, were part of a band that played at musicals and other events around the small communities in north Texas.

As soon as Anna stepped off the bus at the gas station in Ector, Texas, Gustie grabbed her and crushed her in a big hug.

"So glad to see you! How's Papa and Johnnie?"

"They're fine," Anna said. "Papa's busy and Johnnie's a little jealous I came alone."

Gustie laughed. "Well, she can come next time. I've got plans for you."

"What?"

"Oh, just someone I want you to meet."

"Who?" Anna's forehead wrinkled in a small frown.

"You'll see tonight. There's a musical at the gazebo in the park downtown and the Playboys are doing the first set."

A few hours later Anna found herself on the front row of folding chairs, enjoying the warm summer night as the Ector Playboys took the stage.

There was Gustie on piano, Carl on guitar, a tall gangly boy with a fiddle, and a mandolin player with a deep baritone voice and flashing brown eyes. Later, Anna found out his name was Monroe Alderson. The group started out with *Ragtime Cowboy Joe,* exciting the crowd. After a set of western and bluegrass favorites, they swung into the ballad, *I'd Love to Live in Loveland (With a Girl Like You)*.

When the music ended and the crowd began to disperse, Gustie introduced Anna to Monroe first and then to Punk, the fiddler. Anna was instantly attracted to Monroe. He in turn paid quite a bit of attention to her that evening, and for the rest of her visit. Anna couldn't help but notice there were other girls in the crowd who also had eyes for the good-looking singer. Many summer evenings found Anna sitting on someone's lawn listening to Monroe and the band entertain. When they parted at the end of the summer, they promised to write often. Which they did. During the school break at Christmas, Monroe paid a visit to Marietta.

Anna missed her mother every day, but particularly now that she had met Monroe. There were questions she could never ask Papa. Such as, how to make a boy like you as much as you like him. And, how to let a boy know you like him more than any other boy. Anna and Johnnie were popular but certainly not fast. No boy in Marietta was brave enough to try to get fresh with Sam Long's daughters.

To her delight Anna retrieved an envelope addressed to her in Monroe's almost illegible scrawl. She stuck it in her jacket pocket to read later.

Johnnie looked up when Anna entered. The stew left over from last night's supper was warming on the stove.

"Do you want to stir up some cornbread?" she asked as Anna set three plates around the table. Johnnie turned on the radio and rotated the dial until music filled the room.

"I don't think there's time," Anna answered. "Look in the bread box. There may be a couple of pieces — or some biscuits from breakfast. Give the cornbread to Papa. Cold biscuits are fine for me."

"Got a letter from your sweetie?" Johnnie teased.

"Never you mind." Anna smiled. The sisters, less than two years apart in age, were also good friends. And fourteen-year-old Johnnie was incurably romantic.

"A cup of coffee, a sandwich and you-oo," came over the air waves. The girls laughed and joined in, improvising a two-step across the kitchen floor. "A cozy corner, a table for two..."

Sam came through the door that connected to his office. Anna jumped to turn off the radio while Johnnie poured her papa a glass of milk.

With a quick "Hello girls," he strode to the sink, washed his hands and dried them on the dish towel, something he would never have done if Louisa were still alive. He pulled up a cane-bottom chair that looked too flimsy to hold him and sat at the table in front of the steaming bowl of stew. The girls dropped into their chairs and bowed their heads as Sam prayed.

"Forgive our sins, gracious Lord. Make us thankful for these and all thy blessings. In Christ name we pray. Amen."

A bite of stew and cornbread disappeared into Sam's mouth just as the telephone rang.

"Oh, Glory! Will you get that, Anna?"

Anna smiled at her Papa, walked into the hall and took down the receiver.

"Hello, this is the operator. Is this Anna Mae or Johnnie Ruth?"

"This is Anna, Mrs. Jenkinson."

"Well, hello, Anna. How are you today?

"Fine, thank you."

"Anna, will you ask your father to please step over to the bank? There seems to be some trouble."

"Yes, ma'am, I'll tell him. Wha...?"

"Thank you, Anna. I'll see you Sunday."

"Yes, ma'am."

Walking back into the kitchen, Anna wondered what the trouble at the bank might be. Perhaps she should have gotten more information from the operator — and she would have, but Mrs. Jenkinson didn't give her a chance. She let everyone know she didn't like questions. Anna repeated the conversation to Sam. He wiped his mouth with the back of his hand.

"It's probably nothing much. Last week somebody came in raising a ruckus about their account. Threatened to sue the bank for charging interest. Frank called me in to settle the customer down, since he ain't got the backbone to do it himself. I imagine that's what he wants today."

Anna knew there was no love lost between Sam and the bank president, though she wasn't sure why.

Sam shoveled in another couple of bites of stew and said, "Put that on the stove. I'll finish it later." At the door he buckled on his sidearm. "I probably won't need this, but I might drive on out to Thackerville to serve a warrant that come in this morning."

Nineteen

Floyd Hyde watched Olin McCarty speed off on his bike. *Silly kid, going off half-cocked.* Mr. McCarty would likely thank Floyd for keeping Olin out of trouble.

He put up the weapon he had taken from the boy, then stepped behind the counter and continued stocking merchandise. *I'm hungry as a bear. Hope Mr. McCarty don't come back with a list of things for me to do and forgets I ain't had lunch yet.*

Floyd smiled, thinking of Martha and the good lunch she'd sent with him. They'd been married not quite two years and the future held nothing but promise. He couldn't believe his good fortune. Eleven years ago Floyd dropped out of Marietta High School during his last year and joined the Army. His mama had stood crying and waving as the bus left taking him and his two best friends, Harold Smoot and Tommy Don Michaels to boot camp.

They were three young bucks looking for adventure. Let the Kaiser find out about Love County boys. They'd whup his tail good and come back home heroes.

Instead, Harold never came home at all. He lay buried in France — a place called Picardy.

And Tommy Don was left a shell-shocked ghost of a man, sitting in an old soldiers' home.

Floyd fared better, he supposed, with a bullet in his lower back. The Medics at the front told him he'd never walk again, but he fooled them. Hardly a year went by before he was up on his feet. Of course he walked like a baby with a full diaper, but it was a long sight better than crutches or a wheel chair. With all the horrors he'd seen and all that was wrong with him — scars on his face and a funny walk — he figured he'd missed any chance to live a normal kind of life. He took to drinking quite a bit. Going to honky tonks and getting into fights.

Then one night, four years ago, he drove to a bootlegger down on the Red River for a quart of corn liquor. He took his first slug standing by the car talking to a friend and by the time he started back home he was pretty well lit. He was clipping along in the Ford and all of a sudden he saw a tree standing right in the middle of the road.

What's that tree doing in the middle of the road? About that time he hit it. Turned out to be the elm that sat at the end of Third Avenue — on the courthouse lawn.

Sam Long took Floyd inside the jail and put him in a

cell to sleep it off. The next morning he got a breakfast of the best biscuits and gravy he'd ever tasted. He also got a serious talking to.

"What you wasting your life for, Floyd?" The sheriff stood head and shoulders over Floyd, as he did most men. "You go out and get likkered up, try to wrap your car around a tree, and for what good reason? Your mama probably cries every night, watching you turn into a drunken bum."

Floyd, sober for the first time in days, hung his head and said, "I know. You're right, Sheriff. I'm no good."

"Nobody said you're no good. What I said is you're wasting the good you got in you."

"Well, look at me. This is the only life I have. I got no future. I can't walk right. Can't do a man's work. I got nothing to offer nobody and I don't see it ever being any different."

"You gotta quit feeling sorry for yourself. You learned to walk when they said you couldn't. That took grit. Don't tell me you can't change. You can straighten up any time you want to."

And he did. The sheriff's words stayed with Floyd long after his hangover had passed. He left the jail that day a different man.

He'd figured no girl would look at him twice, but Martha was different. When he asked her to marry him, she said yes. He had a good job at McCarty's Hardware making $15.00 a week. He and Martha rented a nice apartment upstairs over Mrs. Campbell's house. Then there was Floydene — a beautiful baby who hardly ever cried, who gripped his finger and laughed when he cooed at her. There were two Grandmamas happy to watch the baby every now and then while he and Martha took in a movie. What more could a man want out of life?

Floyd climbed the ladder to put up a display of brooms and buffing mops. *Wonder what put the bee in Olin's bonnet. Acted pretty sure there was a robbery. Well, I hope not.*

During dinnertime there could be several customers in the bank. Businesses making their deposits, folks taking care of loan payments. A prime time for a robbery, if someone had a mind to do it. But dangerous. People could get hurt.

Maybe I rushed Olin out too soon. Shoulda asked him some questions. Maybe he knew what he was talking about.

Surely Olin called the sheriff, if he thought a robbery was going on. Floyd himself had told Olin that it was the sheriff's business, not theirs. *Wonder if there's a deputy around somewhere? Hate for Sam to take on a gang by himself. I'd give odds on Sam Long against any man living, but if it's a gang, he might need help.*

Floyd took the Winchester from the rack and stuffed extra shells in his jacket pocket. *Maybe I need to go take a look and see what's going on over to the bank. Never thought I'd ever again aim a gun at a human being. But — I gotta help Sam if he needs it.*

He flipped the sign to say 'CLOSED.' Locking the door behind him, he lumbered down the street toward the bank, as fast as possible.

Twenty

Cecil Wooley stood in the lobby of the Love County National Bank wishing he'd never let Jake talk him into this.

Jake had always been able to needle his brother into doing something they shouldn't. Cecil knew better than to listen to Jake's lame-brained ideas — not just because it might be bad, but because if anyone was going to get in trouble, it would be Cecil. Papa always blamed the oldest son for any mischief. Of the two boys, Jake was the leader, not Cecil. When they pushed over the teacher's outhouse on Halloween night, it was Jake's idea. When they set fire to the hay while learning to smoke, it was Jake who had brought home the makings. It was always Jake getting Cecil in trouble, but Virgil never saw it that way.

The minute I heard Jake say 'bank robbery' I shoulda run like a jack rabbit. But no, I ain't got that much sense. I fall right in line. Just like always.

Cecil shifted his weight and looked at the group of

people staring back at him, their eyes full of fear.

Yep, Jake made all the plans. And he planned for me *to stand here and point a gun at these folks.*

"High noon is gonna be the best time to make our move," Jake had said that morning as they put their shotguns in the back seat of Otis' Model T. "Everybody knows Sam Long always takes dinner with his girls over to the jailhouse. With some luck we'll be long gone to Texas before he even finds out what's going on."

"I hope you're right."

"Listen, Cecil. You just keep everyone quiet while I take Eastham to the vault. Don't let anyone leave or get near a phone. That's all you got to do."

Jake parked in front of the bank heading west. There was very little traffic, so he and Cecil climbed out of the car, quickly covered their faces and walked into the bank.

"HEY! Everybody listen!" Jake yelled. "This is a hold-up. You guys come out from those cages and line up. And stick 'em up! No funny business and nobody will get hurt."

He motioned for Cecil to take over watching the lobby. Side-stepping desks and chairs, he met Frank Eastham just as he came out of his office. Jake raised his pistol even with Frank's face.

"You. Mr. High and Mighty Bank President. Turn around. Put your hands up. We're going to the vault. You lead the way nice and easy." He yelled over his shoulder at Cecil, "Stay by the door. And if anyone comes in, you make 'em line up with the others. I'll take care of everything else."

Even though Cecil was nervous, he had to admit things were going along pretty much according to plan. Jake and Mr. Eastham were in the vault loading money into a tow sack. That bag full of money would put the Wooley family on Easy Street.

The customers, tellers, and bookkeepers all stood in front of the teller cages, away from the telephone. Actually, it had been easy so far. He had his papa's pistol in his pocket, but he hadn't had to show it. Jake'd motioned everyone into place and they'd gone without a squawk.

Okay. I can do this. Just take it easy like Jake says. The front door opened and Mattie Lou Hudson stepped into the bank. Cecil swung around, startled. *That girl that works for the Easthams.*

The color drained from Mattie's face and she gave a little "Oh." Cecil jerked his head in the direction of the others. Keeping her eyes on the masked man, Mattie stumbled a little and finally stood in line with the others. Her lip trembled and her eyes filled.

Cecil scanned the group again to make sure everyone was in their place.

What's taking Jake so long? Eastham might be stalling around trying to pull a fast one. Staying away from the windows, Cecil tried to maneuver to the side enough to see into the vault area. This time when the front door burst open, catching him off guard, Cecil nearly jumped out of his skin.

"What's going on in here?" Wendell asked. His voice sounded loud in the hushed quiet of the frightened customers.

Without speaking, Cecil pointed his finger at Wendell and jerked his thumb toward the others. Wendell frowned, looked around, appearing confused. Cecil repeated the gesture.

"What is it, pal?" Wendell said. "What's eating you?"

Cecil drew out the gun. He whacked Wendell lightly on the upper arm and swung the pistol in the direction he wanted Wendell to move.

"Okay, okay." Wendell sauntered across the bank lobby to stand by Mattie Lou. "Don't worry about a thing."

Relieved that the milkman had finally done as he was told, Cecil didn't notice that Wendell wasn't really speaking to him. Instead, he gave the impression he was addressing everyone in the room when he smiled and said, "Everything is copacetic."

Twenty-one

Olin McCarty pedaled toward home. Never had the four blocks felt so long. *I hope Papa's still there. If he's not … Well, I'll just have to figure a way to get my gun past Mama and out of the house. Can I make it back to town in time on this bike — carrying a rabbit gun?*

Olin had no doubt that if he had a weapon he would be able to help the sheriff, maybe even nab a bank robber. The past two summers Olin and Sammy Long had gone to Military Training Camp together where they practiced shooting every day. Both had qualified as sharpshooters.

When he was still a half-block away, Olin saw his papa's car pull out of the driveway and head toward him.

Aaron gave Olin a perfunctory wave as they passed each other going in opposite directions. Olin wheeled his bike into a U-turn and chased after his papa's Olds. Seeing Olin in the rear-vision mirror, Aaron braked and rolled down the window, waiting for Olin to catch up.

"What is it, Son? Did you need something?"

Olin, panting from the fierce pedaling, tried to catch his breath.

"Papa . . . the bank . . ."

"Slow down. I can't get what you're saying. Take a deep breath."

"Someone's robbing the . . . bank . . . I saw them . . . they have . . . guns . . ."

"Did you call the sheriff?"

"Yes. I told Mrs. Jenkinson. She said she'd tell him."

"Okay. Take it easy. He's on his way then." Aaron tipped his hat back and scratched his head. "But he might need help."

"Yes sir, that's what I thought."

"So, what did you think you'd do?"

"I was going to get me a gun and hide behind the pillars in front of the bank and stop the robber when he came out."

"Okay. Get your bike out of the street and get in. We'll need the guns."

"Okay, Papa."

"And, Olin?" The boy paused. "We're not telling your mama about this."

"Yes sir."

Olin entered the back door as quietly as he could. *Oh, shoot. Mama's still in the kitchen. Think fast.*

"Oh, Olin. I just put the food away."

"That's okay, Mama. I — ate already." *At breakfast.* He slid his hand in his jacket pocket and crossed his fingers. "I just need some homework I forgot. I left it in Papa's study."

"All right. You better hurry or you'll be late for your next class."

"Yes, ma'am."

Olin deliberately closed the door as he left the kitchen and met his papa in the front hall. In the study, they retrieved the key from the desk and unlocked the guns. They pulled out Aaron's rabbit gun — a new Marlin lever action .22 — and Olin's smaller Browning .410 shotgun. Olin grabbed two boxes of shells. He closed the front door as his papa climbed into the car. Less than five minutes had passed.

The younger McCarty propped the guns between his legs, barrels resting on his shoulder, as Aaron backed out of the drive and headed toward town.

Twenty-two

Sam Long loved his 1926 four-door Chevrolet, the one extravagance he afforded himself. He always drove with the curtains up, regardless of the weather. He frequently thought of Louisa when he washed or polished the car, bought brand new just weeks before she died.

"Come to the door, Louisa. Look what I got."

"Oh, Sam. You got yourself a new car. It's real pretty."

"Anna, Johnnie," Sam yelled. "Help your mama get her coat on. I'm taking her for a drive." And they rode around Marietta and out Highway 77 toward Red River. *It was a sunny, winter day — kinda like today, and she loved being outdoors.*

"Tell you what, Mama. Let's drive up to Turner Falls."

Louisa looked at him and smiled. "Oh, Sam, I'd love to. But I'm just too tired to ride all that way."

"Maybe today you are. But we'll take off early some morning when you're rested. Just the two of us."

Sam — and Louisa, too — missed East Tennessee. Their home state was vastly different from the flat, windy spaces in Oklahoma. Just north of Ardmore lay the Arbuckle Mountains. Hardly a comparison to the Great Smokies, but they were as close an imitation as one could find in the Sooner State. Sam and Louisa had taken the kids there for outings several times over the years. Their favorite spot was Turner Falls, the site of a 75-foot waterfall, natural pools for swimming and caves to explore.

"Sammy took to swimming like a fish." The big sheriff turned to smile at his wife.

"He sure did. Much better than the girls. They never learned to swim enough to save themselves, but they loved playing in the mountain water. It's so clean up there."

Sam laughed. "Yes, but freezing. Don't know how they stood it."

Louisa smiled. "Kids."

"Are you sure you wouldn't like to go?"

She laid her head against the soft upholstery. "Maybe. We'll see."

"Okay, maybe in the spring."

But Louisa's energy was dwindling quickly, and that was the only ride she took in Sam's new car. It was a good memory.

Sam climbed in the Chevy, engaged the clutch and turned the electric starter. The engine immediately caught. Sam smiled. He'd paid over $500 for this car, an extravagance. But it had never failed to start.

The lawman felt lucky that he'd always been able to take care of his wife and kids and provide them with a few luxuries in addition to their basic needs. The different enterprises and commercial ventures he engaged in had always met a need in the communities where he lived.

Even though I face re-election every four years, this job feels steady. The county is growing. Always need a sheriff to keep the law. May need to put on another deputy next year.

Sam parked just off Main Street on Second Avenue, across from Kelley's Drug, still thinking of his family and counting his blessings.

Anna set to graduate in '29. Probably marry that boyfriend of hers from Texas. Then it'll be only Johnnie at home. Need to think about that. Is it proper for a single young girl to live in the jail?

A Model T Ford sat in front of the bank, its nose pointing west.

Wonder who's on the wrong side of the street? Don't recognize that car.

The sheriff frowned in the winter sunlight, looking intently at the strange vehicle.

Twenty-three

Sam pulled off his gloves and stuffed them in his pocket. His right hand worked on the top button of his coat as he stepped through the door of the bank.

"Mr. Long, we're being robbed!" Earl Simpson, the teller, yelled out as the masked robber whirled to face the sheriff, his gun drawn.

"Old Man, get in line and put your hands up!" The gunman, his face partially covered by a bandana, waved the revolver in Sam's direction.

Sam stopped in his tracks. *Drat. What did that operator tell Anna was going on here? Nothing like this, I'll wager.*

Seven customers, hands in the air, stood frozen with their backs against the teller cages. Sam recognized old Mr. and Mrs. Malvern, Wendell the milkman, and Mattie Lou, Anna Mae's friend. The teller looked like he might faint or throw up. Frank Eastham was nowhere in sight.

Sam continued to work at the button while he raised

his left hand slightly and turned the palm upward. "Hell, *young* man, it's my job to tell you to put *your* hands up."

Mrs. Malvern wept into her hankie; her husband, his arm around her shoulders, eyes glued on the thief, patted her absently. Wendell shifted slightly to stand in front of Mattie Lou.

The outlaw saw the movement and came to life. "You! Be still!" He turned his gun toward Wendell.

Inside the vault, Jake Wooley held his .45 on Frank Eastham while the bank president filled a sack with twenty dollar bills. The safe was not as full as it might have been on the first of the month when extra cash is kept on hand to meet the payrolls around town. But no matter what amount was taken, it would hurt. Frank moved slowly and precisely, trying to keep the masked man in his line of vision.

On the shelf above the stacks of twenties sat a metal cash box. Inside it Frank had put a .22 caliber revolver — for a time such as this. A bank officer in Kansas City fooled a robber into thinking the box held large bills — hundreds. The banker opened the box, grabbed the hidden gun and shot the thief. Frank dropped the banded bills into the sack, watching and waiting to make his move.

In the lobby, the outlaw turned his pistol on Wendell. Sam stepped to the side and lowered his right hand to his gun belt. The thief whirled and fired two shots in the general direction of where the lawman had been standing. Sam dropped to his right knee and took careful aim. By the time Cecil Wooley hit the floor, he was dead with a bullet in his heart.

The sound of gunfire reverberated through the vault. "What the hell ...?" Jake yelped. He jerked around, facing the door. Before Frank could react, Jake turned back, leveling the barrel at Frank's torso. "Get over against that wall and don't move."

Frank backed up until he touched the file cabinet in the back of the vault — even farther away from the cash box that held the .22. Jake grabbed the half-full sack. He stole a look into the main area of the bank just as the Sheriff took a step toward the downed Cecil to remove his mask.

Jake, his face still covered, bolted from the vault, shooting. His first shot blazed through Sam's thick coat and nicked the flesh of his upper left arm. Sam felt the bullet's sting and returned fire, emptying his revolver at the charging gunman.

The shooting stopped. Silence fell on the lobby as Sam Long sank to the floor.

Carrying a tow sack, the masked outlaw stepped around the end of the counter he had used for cover and stood over the sheriff, who was bleeding from a wound in his side.

"You — son of a bitch!" Jake Wooley glared down at the man he hated. He calmly leveled his revolver at Sam and squeezed the trigger. The click of the hammer on the empty chamber echoed throughout the bank. Mattie Lou's scream pierced the air as old Mrs. Malvern dropped to the floor in a dead faint, taking her husband, who tried to catch her, down with her. Jake Wooley spit at the fallen lawman, coolly stepped over his brother's body and trotted out the door.

In the vault, Frank hesitated, listening. He leapt across the vault, retrieved the gun and, taking a deep breath, stepped out quickly and surveyed the scene. The sheriff, one of the robbers and two customers lay on the floor. The thief carrying the tow sack of money was just clearing the front door.

Sam tried to pull himself to his feet. He had no idea how many bullets he had taken. He only knew his gut burned like fire.

Wendell gathered Mattie in his arms. One more scream, muffled by his chest, and she was quiet. "It's okay, Mattie. It's okay. You're okay. Everything's all right now."

He held her face in his hands for a moment then kissed her tenderly on each cheek. "Stand here while I see about Mr. Long."

The sheriff gave a low grunt, trying to rise. Wendell rushed to kneel at his side.

"Sheriff, are you okay?" The front of Sam's shirt was soaked with blood.

"Help me get up, Wendell. I'm hit, but I can walk . . ."

Gently but firmly, Wendell made an effort to help the lawman to his feet. Sam struggled to rise but when he gave out a growl of pain, Wendell lowered him to the floor.

"Let's try it again . . ." Sam's voice trailed off and his eyes closed.

"Earl!" Wendell yelled, yanking the muffler from his neck and wadding it against Sam's stomach. "Go get Doc Autry. Hurry!"

The bank teller flew out the front door to the doctor's office across the street above Kelley's. Frank Eastham strode to his office and picked up the phone.

"Number please."

"Ring over to James Randolph's house." Frank sounded as winded as if he had run a race.

"Yes, Mr. Eastham. Is there trouble?" Mrs. Jenkinson's used her most businesslike voice, appropriate for speaking to an important man. "Did Sheriff Long come over like I asked him to? If he's not there yet, that Anna girl must not . . ."

"Dammit, Inez, mind your business and get Jim Randolph over here right away. We need a lawman!"

For the first time in her life, Inez Jenkinson could think of nothing to say.

When Dr. Autry reached the bank a few minutes later, Sheriff Sam Long of Love County lay unconscious on the floor.

Twenty-Four

Mattie Lou Hudson inched backward until she touched the teller's cage. Her hand over her mouth, stifling new outcries, she watched Wendell try to help Sheriff Long. This was her best friend's papa! With his blood pooling on the floor of the bank, despite Wendell's efforts to staunch it. *Can anyone hurt that bad live over it?*

Mattie took a deep breath, trying to compose herself. She couldn't believe what she had witnessed. A gun battle! A man shot to death and another wounded.

Most of all, she was amazed at Wendell. She had never seen him like this. *Wasn't he afraid? He stood between me and the gunman. He did that on purpose. He didn't back down. And when everyone else panicked, he held me and told me I would be okay.*

Makes me feel protected.

And loved.

Twenty-Five

Floyd was just crossing Front Avenue, still two blocks from the bank, when he saw Aaron McCarty's car approaching from the south. Olin sat in the passenger seat. *Okay. I'm fired. I interfered with Olin, then I locked up the store and left. Now, I'm carrying a gun that doesn't belong to me.*

The large car pulled up at the corner and stopped. Aaron rolled down the window and yelled, "Floyd?"

"Y-yes sir."

"You on your way to the bank?"

"Yes sir!"

"Well, hop on."

Floyd jumped on the running board, stuck his arm through the open window and grabbed hold. As Aaron turned onto Main Street, he saw, down in the next block, a man walk quickly out of the bank. The bill of the man's hat was pulled down to hide the upper part of his face; the neckerchief he wore covered his mouth and chin. He carried a cloth sack. He looked around then hurriedly walked toward a Model T Tudor pointed in their direction.

Aaron slowed his vehicle.

"Floyd, you got a plan?"

"I hadn't thought much about it, sir. I figured I'd know when the time come."

Aaron took a deep breath. "Well, we can't talk it over right now. Looks like he's heading this way. Floyd, I'm gonna let you out at the corner. You shoot at his tires and try not to hit the gas tank. Olin and I will double back down the alley and head him off before he gets to the tracks."

Aaron gunned the big motor and sped forward. He slowed to let Floyd jump off at 2nd Avenue, then turned down the alley that ran parallel to Main.

Floyd forced his weak legs to move. As he saw the robber's car pull away from the curb, he tucked the butt of the rifle in his shoulder, took aim and fired. Chips of brick flew up when the bullet missed the tire and dug into the street. As the Ford passed him gaining speed, he fired again, this time hitting the mark. He watched the back tire explode just as Aaron and Olin stepped into the street a few yards ahead of the escaping thief. Olin let go a load of buckshot aimed at the front end of the car.

Even from where he stood, Floyd could see the smoke rise when the radiator took a direct hit. The car swerved to the right, crossed the sidewalk and hit the street light on the corner. The thief's pulled-down hat and turned up collar provided little protection from the shotgun pellets or the windshield's flying glass. He pulled himself out of the car to face the McCartys, father and son, standing with guns leveled at his chest.

When Deputy Randolph screeched down Main Street in his little coupe, he found a crowd huddled around the outside of the bank. Farther down the street, a Tudor Sedan sat blocking the sidewalk. The light pole at Main and Fourth lay across the hood. Jake Wooley, his robber's bandana around his neck, his hands in the air, stood unsteadily beside the car. He was in the custody of Olin and Aaron McCarty, flanked by Floyd Hyde.

Twenty-Six

Anna and Johnnie finished washing the lunch dishes, leaving them to drain dry. While Johnnie covered Papa's bowl of stew and set it on the back of the stove for later, Anna slipped into the bathroom.

She ran a comb through her short hair that fell just under her ears, smoothed the straight bangs and dabbed a bit of color on her lips and cheeks. Sitting on the edge of the tub, she opened Monroe's letter.

Dear Anna Mae,

How are you? Fine I hope. I am fine, too.

I had fun at Christmas. I can't wait till you can come see Gustie and Carl again. When do you think you will come to Texas again?

Well, be good. Don't do anything I wouldn't do.

Love,

Monroe

P.S. The band is playing next weekend at a revival at the Baptist Church in Tom Ball. Wish you could be there. RMA

Anna ran her fingers over the page, lingering over the word 'love.' *Does he mean that? Or is he a flirt who says 'love' to all the girls?* She raised the paper to her lips and kissed the signature, leaving a tell-tale bit of lip rouge. Closing her eyes she conjured up Monroe's face, his big smile, his beautiful voice, and teasing eyes. *Oh, I love him. I do. I wish I knew for sure how he feels. If only . . .*

"Anna! Come *on!*" Johnnie's knuckles banged on the door. "We'll be late to school if you don't get a wiggle on. Everything's done in the kitchen — no thanks to my love-sick sister."

"Oh, hush up." Anna hurried through the house grabbing her coat and cap. "We'll make it in plenty of time. Just wait till someone makes your heart stand still. Then you'll understand."

The two girls hurried along in the winter sunshine, laughing and talking. As they crossed Seminole Street in front of Roper's funeral home, the ambulance raced out of the drive with Tim Roper at the wheel. At the end of the block, the siren blared and the long vehicle turned toward downtown.

There was time for only one curious look at the ambulance as the girls rushed on and crossed the lawn in front of the high school. Just as they climbed the twelve cement steps to the door, the first bell rang.

"Oh, golly," Johnnie said, "We're in the duck soup for sure. *Run.*"

The two scampered through the heavy doors and walked-ran to their respective classes. Anna had Spanish the first hour after lunch. Miss Campbell was a real bear when someone was late. The sound of the last bell echoed through the now-almost-empty halls as Anna quickened her step and let the door shut just as the ringing stopped.

"Glad you could make it, Señorita Long. Take your seat, please."

Miss Campbell turned her back to the classroom and methodically erased the blackboard. She walked to the large trashcan in the corner of the room and clapped the erasers together sharply, causing chalk dust to fly. She then returned the erasers to their respective holders.

"Class, I am feeling particularly benevolent today. I will give you fifteen minutes to check the homework you were assigned for last night — or to *finish* the homework assigned. It will not be necessary for you to discuss this with your neighbor. As a matter of fact, if you value your free time after school, I would seriously discourage such conversation."

Anna turned quickly to the page she had worked on last night. The assignment: Translate the following paragraph into Spanish. She checked the page line by line. She was sure the work was correct. Dreamily, she doodled on a blank page in her notebook.

Como te amo? How do I love thee?

She scarcely heard the door open but raised her head at the quiet mention of her name. The fourth-hour office aide stood beside Miss Campbell's desk.

"Miss Anna Long, you're wanted in Mr. Griffin's office." Anna's stomach tightened as she heard a sharp intake of breath from several students in the room. Anna Mae Long was *never* called to the principal's office. She laid her pencil on the desk and rose.

"Take your things with you."

Anna gathered her notebook and jacket. *What on earth? Rats! The principal or one of his snitches must have seen me scooting lickety-split.* She stepped into the hall and saw Johnnie up ahead, walking toward the office. *Oh, boy. I guess they nabbed her, too.* Anna caught up and the sisters exchanged side-long glances as they entered the principal's office.

Mr. Griffin stood in the door to his private office. "Come in, girls. Sit down." He didn't look nearly as scary as he did in assembly when he was reminding students to obey school rules. He stood in front of his desk and waited a long moment before he spoke.

"I'm sorry to tell you this, girls, but there's been a shooting at the bank. It seems the sheriff walked into an ambush. He's been shot."

Anna sat straight up. "Shot? No!" It was almost a scream. "What happened? When Papa left, he said it was probably nothing. Where is he?" She turned to Johnnie, whose mouth formed a small 'o', her eyes wide and frightened.

"You knew he was going to the bank?" Mr. Griffin asked.

"The — the operator called . . ."

"She called your papa to the bank? What did she say — when she called?"

"She said, 'Will you ask your father to please go over to the bank? There seems to be some trouble.'"

"Didn't she say something about robbers inside the bank?"

"No. Nothing. And Papa said it was probably nothing." Tears filled Anna's eyes and ran freely down her face.

"Let me hasten to tell you — your papa is alive. But he is seriously wounded."

Anna collapsed against the back of the chair. She put both hands over her face and shook her head rapidly. "No. No. No. No."

Johnnie Ruth, sitting beside Anna, had frozen at the first word. Now, she turned to look at her sister.

"Are you sure you heard right, Anna Mae?" Johnnie said.

Anna emitted a low moan. Her body rocked, bouncing gently against the chair arms.

"There, there." Mr. Griffin moved closer and patted

Anna on the shoulder. "Your papa's in the ambulance on his way to the sanitarium in Ardmore. Mr. and Mrs. McCarty are taking you there. We'll be checking on you later. Be strong, now. Your papa will need you to be strong."

Anna stood, wiping tears from her face with both hands as Mr. Griffin escorted the two girls to the door. In a daze, she let herself be put into the back seat of Aaron McCarty's Oldsmobile. Johnnie, in stunned silence, climbed in beside her.

As they left Marietta and headed up Highway 77 to Ardmore, Johnnie asked Anna the question she would have to answer over and again during the next few months. The question she would hear from law enforcement, her family, the well-meaning and the curious: "Just exactly what did the operator say to you?"

Twenty-Seven

Aaron McCarty's car stopped in front of the two-story brick building that was Hardy Sanitarium. Doctor Walter Hardy established this hospital in 1911 as the most modern medical center in southern Oklahoma, with three doctors on staff and round-the-clock nurses.

"Okay, girls. We're here," Aaron said, turning off the engine. "Now, you might not be able to see your papa right away. But we'll find a doctor or nurse to tell us how he's doing."

Clinging tightly to one another, Anna and Johnnie walked up the few steps and through the heavy double doors. The smell of carbolic assaulted their senses.

"You wait here," Aaron said. "I'll find out what I can."

Mary McCarty ushered the two girls into the waiting room, hovering over them like a hen with one chick.

"I've been praying the whole way for your papa," she said. "You must pray, too. He's a strong man. God will see him through this."

After fifteen minutes that felt like hours, Aaron came into the waiting area. Anna and Johnnie jumped up.

"Sam's alive! They're still working on him. The bullet is in his stomach or chest somewhere. They're taking an x-ray. Very serious. But Doctor Hardy is here. So you know Sam's in the best hands. There's nothing for us to do now, but wait."

Johnnie sank into the nearest chair. Anna paced the room until Mary convinced her to sit beside Johnnie.

Anna fetched a handkerchief from her pocket and wiped her eyes. She twisted the bit of linen in her hands. *What should I have done differently when Mrs. Jenkinson called? I started to ask what the trouble was, but she cut me off. Like it was none of my business. So I thought maybe it wasn't.*

"The robber was caught, by the way," Aaron spoke up. "We . . ."

"Aaron. Let's don't talk about that," Mary said gently.

"Why not? Might make the girls feel better. Though I don't know much more than that. When Deputy Randolph pulled up I left to come get you. I figured Olin could fill Jim in on what happened."

"Olin?! What was Olin . . . ?"

". . . uh, you're right, Mary. We can talk about this later."

A nurse came in with a tray holding a coffee pot and four mugs. Mary busied herself trying to get Johnnie and

Anna to sip some of the hot drink. Anna numbly accepted the cup and walked to the large window to look out on the late afternoon traffic in the small city.

Jim Randolph strode in from outside, bringing a rush of cold air.

"Good afternoon, Mr. McCarty, Mrs. McCarty, ladies," he said, tipping his hat in the girls' direction. "Is there any news about the Sheriff? I tried to telephone but couldn't get any sense out of whoever answered."

Aaron caught him up on what information he had. The deputy nodded.

"Well, while we're waiting here, I wonder if I could talk to Anna and Johnnie."

The sisters sat side by side on two straight-backed chairs, facing the deputy.

"Now, from what little information I've been able to gather, Olin McCarty told Mrs. Jenkinson someone was robbing the bank and she called the sheriff. Is that right, girls? Did Sam get such a call that you know of?"

"Yes sir," Johnnie said. "Anna answered the phone."

"Okay, Miss Anna. So you gave Sam the message about the robbery."

"No, sir. . ."

"You didn't?"

"No — I mean, the operator didn't tell me. . . "

"Are you sure? She swears she told you there was trouble at the bank."

"She did. I mean — that's what she said. 'There's trouble.' She didn't say there was a robbery going on."

"Are you sure?"

"Of course, I'm sure. Don't you think I would have told Papa if she had said any such thing?"

"Don't use a smart tone to your elders, Anna," Mary interjected quietly.

"I'm sorry. But — really, I'm trying to remember. . ."

"Okay." Jim Randolph pulled a chair in front of Anna and sat so near their knees almost touched. "Let's start all over. What happened when the phone rang?"

"Papa said, 'O Glory. Will you get that, Anna?'" Johnnie blurted.

"Okay. Let's let Miss Anna answer, please."

Johnnie slumped against the back of her chair.

"So you answered the phone, Anna. Then what?"

"Mrs. Jenkinson asked who she was talking to and I told her."

"Then what did she say?"

"She said would the sheriff come over to the bank, there was some trouble."

"She didn't say what the trouble was?"

"No, I started to ask . . ."

"Didn't you think it strange for the sheriff to be called to the bank on his lunch hour if it wasn't something important?"

"I didn't think . . ."

"Well, think now, Anna. Tell me again what Mrs. Jenkinson said."

Anna paused, took a deep breath, trying to concentrate on memorizing every word of the conversation with the telephone operator.

"She said, 'Will you tell the sheriff to go over to the bank, there's some trouble.'"

"And she didn't say what kind of trouble?"

"No — I — I'm sure she didn't."

"Did she say anything else?"

"Something about seeing me in church . . ." Throughout the telling, tears poured down Anna's face; now she hiccupped a big sob and fell sideways against Johnnie.

"Okay, that's enough. We'll talk more later."

Jim Randolph was returning the chairs to their original places when Dr. Hardy appeared at the door.

"Sheriff Long's family?"

Jim swung around. "Yes, Doctor. I'm his deputy. These are his daughters. And Mr. and Mrs. McCarty."

The doctor inclined his head slightly in greeting to

the group and spoke to the deputy. "The sheriff is resting now. You can see him in an hour or so. The bullet went through his stomach and is lying against his spine in a precarious position. We have decided not to remove it at this time. We found during the war that a man could live with a bullet in his body and sometimes that was a better choice than risking surgery. When Mr. Long is stronger, we may consider surgery again, but at this time it's not wise."

"Oh, thank you, Lord," Mary whispered.

"When can I see him?" During the doctor's report, Anna had risen from her chair and now stood in front of Dr. Hardy, her hands clasped as though pleading. "I need to see him."

"In about an hour, Child." The doctor patted her shoulder. "Right now, your papa is alive — and doing as well as can be expected."

Twenty-Eight

Monroe Alderson tilted his head toward the mandolin, plucked each of the dual strings and twisted a peg –just a hair. He strummed across the strings, played a series of chords. *Perfect.*

Every Tuesday in Ector, Texas, was music night at the Locke's house. It started early with band practice for the four musicians who played together for various occasions. Monroe, Carl, Gustie and Punk were gaining a reputation around Fannin County. There wasn't a dance, party or wedding, revival or singing convention — even funeral — where the Ector Playboys weren't eager to share their talents. They knew every song in the Cokesbury Hymnal and many more from the Heavenly Highways songbook, along with all the old ballads and the current ragtime favorites. The band was invited to almost any event that needed a good musical group.

Band practice wasn't a chore — the four loved playing together. After a couple of hours of rehearsal, friends began to stop by. Some brought their own instruments so they might join in. If the weather was nice they gathered on the front porch and lawn. In the winter months, as many as possible crowded into Gustie's living room.

Gustie, the only female 'Playboy,' read music but also played by ear. This enabled her to pick up new songs easily and transpose to another key if necessary. Monroe was expert on mandolin and guitar, lead singer, and front man. Carl acted as manager, booking dates for the group and playing second guitar. Punk handled back-up singing and fiddling. He was not nearly as talented as the others — still, he and Monroe had been pals since they were in diapers, so Punk had a place in the band.

Monroe's parents, Charlie and Hattie, were proud of him for his ability with stringed instruments. While he was still young enough to carry the nickname 'Little Boy' he could hear the harmony in a tune. In his early teens, now simply called 'Boy' by his parents and sisters, Monroe learned to sight-read music using the 7-scale shape note system. Shape notes, taught in the singing schools of the day, used a series of triangles, circles, trapezoids and squares to represent the root 'do' of the scale and all the other tones. Monroe was an excellent sight-reader. If he didn't know the song requested, he could quickly learn it — if it were transcribed into shapes.

Charlie and Hattie encouraged the singing schools and conventions, but looked askance at the secular tunes.

Charlie sat Monroe down one day to talk about it.

"Boy, you know the Good Lord gave you your musical gift."

"I know, Papa."

"It's because of Him you're so quick at it. Can pick up any tune. Can play so well."

"Yes sir."

"The Good Lord gave you a fine ear. He's given you opportunities to play and sing for some big crowds. Someday, more chances may come your way. Maybe even a chance to earn fame and fortune through your talent."

"I hope so, Papa."

"Tell me the truth, now. Do they have beer and hooch at these parties you play at?"

"No, Papa. I never saw any."

"Well, one day someone might offer you a drink. Don't you take it, Boy."

"I won't."

"I'd be mighty disappointed. And, Son, I'd like for you to watch what kind of songs that band of yours sings. Don't be singing any more of those suggestive or vulgar words."

"No, Papa. I don't play that sort of stuff." Monroe was dumbfounded.

"I heard you the other day out on the porch, you and

Punk. I heard those feisty words."

"Papa, I swear I don't know what you're talking about."

"You and Punk were singing, 'While you're dreaming, I'll be scheming. *You know what I mean.*'" Charlie looked Monroe in the eye and pointed his finger. "Well, *I* know what you mean, and I'll not have it. There's plenty of good gospel songs."

Monroe knew better than to argue back.

"Yes sir," he said. "I'll watch it from now on."

A few minutes before 5:00 that Tuesday afternoon in January, his instruments tuned and in their cases, Monroe stood in the bathroom pulling a comb through his tangled curls. He poured hair oil into his palm, rubbed his hands together and massaged his scalp. After a few minutes of this treatment, combing was much easier, and his hair lay parted and in place. He put the bottle of Vaseline Hair Tonic, a Christmas gift, back on the shelf and looked again in the mirror. Satisfied, he hurried out the door and down the street to band practice.

He covered the two blocks in just a few minutes, singing under his breath, "I'm in love with you, Honey." *Hope she got my letter today. Hope she isn't stepping out with some Fancy Dan up there in Oklahoma.* He stopped. *No, she wouldn't do that. She didn't* say *she loves me, but when I said it to her, she kinda nestled on my shoulder...* Monroe smiled at the pleasant memory. He lengthened his stride and hurried to his destination. "I'm in love with you, *Anna.* Say you love me, too, *Anna. . . .*"

As he stepped onto the Locke's front porch carrying an instrument case in each hand, Gustie opened the front door. "Hi, Mon. Come on in."

"Yoo hoo, Gustie. Wait a minute." Mrs. Hightower, the Locke's neighbor, came rushing across the front yard. "Gustie, honey, come quick. It's your sister — *long distance.*"

Monroe turned. "Anna Mae?"

Gustie jumped off the porch and broke into a run, following Mrs. Hightower to answer the telephone. The screen door opened again as Carl asked, "What's going on?"

"A long distance phone call." Monroe stood looking after the two women. "I hope nothing bad happened."

Twenty-Nine

Sam Long heard the door open softly. He tried to raise his head off the pillow as Jim Randolph walked to the side of his hospital bed.

"Lay still, now Sam. How you doing?"

"My gut hurts like hell."

"Yeah. You caught a bullet."

"I know."

"We nabbed the S.O.B."

"Jess Wooley?"

"Yeah. How did you know?"

"Recognized his voice when he stood over me. And cussed me. His gun misfired or I'd be dead."

"Well, thank God for that."

"I guess the one I dropped was his brother Cecil."

"Yeah. He's dead."

"I figured. Their pa Virgil wasn't mixed up in it, was he?"

"It don't look like it — at least not right now. They was driving a car with Texas plates. Don't know where they got it." The deputy shifted from one foot to the other. "Sorry you walked into an ambush, Sam."

"Couldn't be helped."

"Yeah — well ... I just gotta ask you, Sam — why did you take them on when they had the drop on you?"

"Aww. I just couldn't stand to let them get away with robbing the bank. I thought there might be another one in the vault, but I figured I could take 'em both. I'm a good shot."

"Yeah, I reckon so."

"Did they get away with any money?"

"Naw. The tow sack was still in the car when I — uh, we caught up with him."

"How much?"

"$9,000."

"Lordy." Sam moved his head on the pillow again. "Are my girls here?"

"Yeah. They're just outside. Aaron and Mrs. McCarty drove them up."

"Well, hell, man, bring them in. You oughta know I want to see my girls."

Jim Randolph started to say something else, then turned and left the room. In a moment Johnnie burst in and ran to Sam's bedside, leaving Anna standing just inside the door.

"Oh, Papa. Are you all right?" Johnnie touched his pale face. "Of course you're not. You've been shot. But — does it hurt real bad?"

"I'll be okay. Did you girls thank Mr. McCarty for driving you here?"

"Yes, sir." Johnnie walked back to the door where Anna still stood and caught her hand. Johnnie whispered, "I can't remember if I said thanks or not — so remind me when we get back in the car. Come on over and speak to Papa. What's the matter with you?"

Anna walked slowly to stand by the bed. Trembling, she took Sam's hand in both of hers.

"Hello, Papa." He squeezed her hand in reply. The big man tried to roll his body toward the girls. He grimaced, relaxed, then turned his head on the pillow to look at them.

"Johnnie, will you go find someone and see if I can have a drink of water?"

"Sure, Papa," the young teen replied. She scooted out of the room in search of a nurse.

As the door shut, Anna bent and rested her forehead on their clasped hands. "I'm sorry, Papa."

"Anna, what did Inez Jenkinson say to you?"

Anna raised her head to meet his eyes. "I've been wracking my brain to remember. Honest. She said could you come to the bank, there was trouble."

"Did she say what kind of trouble?"

"I'm almost sure she didn't. In fact I started to ask her and she rang off."

"Did she say anything like the word 'robber' or 'holdup'?"

Tears swimming in Anna's eyes spilled over and ran down her cheeks.

"No, Papa. I know I would have told you. I have to admit that the more I think about it the more confused I get and it's hard to remember all the exact words. But, Papa — if she had said anything like that, I would have told you." She clutched his arm. *"Please! Believe me!"*

"Good gravy, girl. Of course, I believe you. Inez is a meddlesome old biddy. You've got more common sense than she'll ever have. And more character. If it comes down to who to believe, there's no question."

Anna laid her head on the bed near his shoulder. She put her arm across his body, careful to not put weight on his wound. It was the nearest thing to a hug she could manage. He reached across his heavily bandaged chest to stroke her head.

"When I get out of here, I'll find out what happened. And if Inez Jenkinson sent me to that bank without a warning, then — she won't be so full of herself when I get through with her."

Thirty

As Anna and Johnnie lay side by side on the feather bed in the McCarty's guest bedroom, Anna reached over and touched Johnnie's hand. Their fingers twined, they stared at the ceiling, each crying silently.

Neither of the girls had wanted to leave the hospital; both insisted they would be just fine there in the waiting room. But, the doctor had reappeared to tell them that the sheriff was resting well and Mary and Aaron convinced them they should get some rest and come back tomorrow.

"We gave him morphine for the pain. He is sleeping now," Dr. Hardy said. "Rest is the best thing for him. We just need to pray that his wound doesn't get infected. There's no point in anyone staying overnight."

Both McCartys had insisted the girls not go back to their home. Jake Wooley had been patched up by Doctor Autry and put in jail. Jim Randolph or another deputy would bunk in one of the empty cells and keep an eye on him. It would not be prudent for the girls to stay in the downstairs apartment.

It was well after dark when Mary warmed the ham and beans left over from lunch and set them on the table. The baking hen she had planned to have for supper sat in the icebox half-cooked. To be salvaged later, if possible.

At supper, Olin was still full of the excitement he had been a part of that day, but had stern orders from his father not to mention the bank robbery in front of Sheriff Long's girls. For some reason, he felt obliged to keep a conversation going, so he chattered on about his morning English class and Bobo Leaks' antics, while Anna and Johnnie smiled politely. The day's school activities seemed like a different world, a world that no longer was.

When Mrs. McCarty excused them from helping to clean the dishes, they accepted the reprieve without even the mildest protestation. They retreated to their assigned room, thankful to be alone at last.

"This is what Mama was always afraid of," Anna said.

Johnnie turned her head on the pillow. "Was she really? I never heard her say anything like that."

"You were too little. She didn't say much to me either, I overheard them talking."

"When?"

"One night, Papa had gone over to Madill to arrest

someone he had a warrant on. The Madill police had picked this man up for being drunk. When they found out there were serious charges in Love County, they called Papa to come get him. He didn't get back till after supper. You and I had gone to bed. You were probably asleep already, but I heard Papa come in."

"And you eavesdropped?"

"No! Well, maybe. Anyway I was curious, so I listened to the story Papa told Mama. He said when he signed the man out from the Madill police, he decided he'd better search him. Papa's deputy said there was no need for that. He'd been in jail. He couldn't possibly have a weapon."

"So what happened?"

"Papa felt in the con's sock and found a table knife honed down sharp as a razor. He would've stabbed Papa first chance he got."

"Gosh!"

"Yeah. Well, Mama had a fit. Said she had a feeling something bad was going to happen to Papa in this job. Made him promise to be more careful. He said he'd tell her no more tales if she planned to worry so."

Johnnie gave a little laugh. "She could sure get onto him, couldn't she?"

Anna smiled. "She sure could."

"But they sure loved each other, didn't they." Johnnie's eyes filled with tears once again.

Anna rolled toward Johnnie and threw her arm around her. "They sure did."

"Maybe Mama's up in heaven watching out for Papa — and for us."

Anna raised up on her other elbow and looked at her younger sister. "Johnnie, you know I'm telling the truth..." A sob caught in her throat and she couldn't finish.

"Oh, Anna. Please don't cry about that. I'm sorry I asked or even wondered. It wasn't your fault. You didn't know."

Johnnie gathered Anna in her arms and the two sisters lay there together, the younger one comforting the older. As their sobs subsided, Johnnie loosened herself from Anna's grasp to retrieve two handkerchiefs from the dresser top. She climbed back onto the bed and sat cross-legged beside Anna.

"Anna Mae," she said solemnly, "as long as we live I will never again ask you about that telephone call. I promise."

Thirty-One

Anna glanced up as her brother Arthur entered the church parlor.

"The place is full out there." He spoke to no one in particular. Arthur, second from the oldest son and 16 years older than Anna, was the most settled of Sam and Louisa's children. He'd taken work with an oil company in Pampa, Texas as a young man and in time he married and started a family. Arthur was the one to make all the funeral arrangements.

The mayor, Aaron McCarty, and the Board of County Commissioners had prevailed upon the family to have the funeral in the larger Baptist church to accommodate the crowd, even though Sheriff Sam Long was a Methodist. There were no objections from the Long family. Certainly not from Anna. She couldn't stand the thought of sitting in the front pew of First Methodist, where they sat every Sunday, while Sam lay in state just in front of the altar . . . Would she ever be able to sit in that church — in *their* pew — again? Could she worship there without reliving the memory of her papa's funeral?

Arthur made the final decision. While living in Shady Dale they attended a community church, and most of the older boys considered themselves Baptists. The Methodist pastor, Brother Fleming, and Brother Healey from First Baptist would both take part in the service. Folks from all across Love County would gather to mourn their fallen hero.

My whole life will be different now.

When she entered Kelley's Drug Emporium yesterday just as Mr. Kelley was mixing an antiseptic for someone, the smell of phenol attacked Anna's nose — reminding her sharply of the Hardy Sanitarium, where Sam had spent his last days.

And this morning, the sweet aroma from the banks of flowers in the sanctuary was overwhelming. A contrast in odors, but each bringing a painful memory.

Would she ever again hear the ringing of a telephone and not be gripped with fear and dread? The peal that called her papa to the bank. The knell before Dr. Hardy said the dreaded word: pneumonia.

Could she ever again cook Papa's favorite food? She would forever miss his teasing about her kitchen skills. Would there ever come a day when she was not crushed with the loss of this great man she loved so much?

Anna was not able to speak to Inez Jenkinson when the operator stopped by the McCarty's to bring an apple pie. Anna excused herself quickly and left the room, afraid she might say something harsh. Could she ever bring herself to forgive that woman for her part in the circumstances that cost Sam his life?

Brother Fleming stepped in from the hall and spoke softly to Arthur.

"We're waiting for our sister Augusta and her husband," Arthur answered. "They are driving from Texas and should be here any minute. We won't start the service without them."

Oh, Arthur sounds so much like Papa. His speech and mannerisms — the way he takes charge — it's like having Papa here in the room.

"Anna?" Mattie Lou's voice broke through Anna's thoughts.

"Oh, Mattie. I'm so glad you came," Anna said, and began to cry. Mattie put her arms around her friend. The two girls stood rocking together in their grief. After a few minutes they pulled apart and Anna was surprised to see Wendell Allen standing nearby.

"Hello, Wendell. Thank you for coming by."

"I'm really sorry, Anna."

"I heard you were at the bank. You tried to help."

"Wasn't much I could do. Sheriff Long was a good man. Cowards ambushed him. He didn't know there was one in the vault. Nobody had a chance to warn him afore Jake came busting out shooting."

"Thank you anyway — for trying to help."

"Don't mention it. Uh … ah …" He tilted his head in Mattie's direction. "You ready, Mattie Lou? We need to find a seat."

Anna turned quickly and looked at her friend. "Mattie?" And then softly, "Wendell?"

Mattie gave Anna a quick hug and whispered, "I'll tell you all about it later."

Anna watched as Wendell gently touched the crook of Mattie's elbow to guide her out of the room.

Well. Who would've thought? But they do look cute together.

The parlor door opened again and Gustie and Carl burst into the room.

"Sorry we're late — we had a flat. Thanks for waiting."

The couple walked around the parlor, affectionately greeting family they had not seen recently. Squeezing her older sister, Anna looked over Gustie's shoulder and noticed Monroe standing in the doorway. He touched his fingers to his cap, giving Anna a little smile. Then he bared his head, stepped into the room and worked his way around the crowd of people greeting Gustie and Carl.

Anna disengaged from Gustie, turned toward Monroe and took two steps forward, her heart racing, hardly believing her eyes. Monroe covered the distance between them and boldly folded her in his arms, right there in front of her entire family.

"You came," she said.

She nestled her head in the warmth of his shoulder before remembering where they were and who might be watching. Stepping back from his embrace and catching his hands in hers, she said, "I didn't know you were coming, but I'm so glad you did."

"We saw all the flags at half-mast as we drove through town. That's quite an honor."

"Yes. And Mr. Griffin from the high school will conduct the Masonic rites at the gravesite. Papa'll be buried next to Mama."

Brother Fleming appeared at the door again and Arthur said, "We're ready now."

Anna looked around, saw Johnnie and beckoned to her. With her sister on one side and Monroe on the other, she took her place with the family on the front pew of the church.

Brother Fleming stood in the pulpit.

"We have gathered this morning to remember our brother, Samuel Calvin Long, and mourn the loss of his life. He was a true friend of the people. Struck down in the line of duty. Protecting innocent customers in that bank, Brothers and Sisters. He had no warning of impending harm. He had no time to prepare. But to a man like Sam Long that didn't matter. If he had known he was walking into an ambush, Sam would have gone anyway. Because he was a man who did his duty. He was sworn to keep the law and he took that vow seriously. The law was his life. He was a Christian and a Mason. A man of high integrity. He died a hero's death." The pastor opened the Bible in front of him. "I will be reading this morning from the Gospel according to John." He paused, pulled a kerchief from his pocket and wiped his face.

"'Greater love hath no man than this: that a man lay down his life for a friend.'"

Thirty-Two

Anna sat on the sofa in the McCarty's parlor. Aaron and Mary had tactfully vacated the room so Anna and her brother could talk. Arthur Long, nicknamed Ott by his family, paced in front of the fireplace. Johnnie peeked in the door and when beckoned, came to sit beside Anna.

"I don't see how in the world you think you're going to live unless you come to Pampa with us," Arthur said, turning to face his young sisters. Ott had followed the oil rigs to West Texas, earned good money and invested well. Now, in his middle 30s, he and his family were settled.

"I — I — want to go to school …" Anna said, her voice so soft it could barely be heard.

"You can go to school in Texas! What do you lack? Another year? You can go to school. Johnnie, too."

"Ott, the McCartys said we could stay with them till the end of the term."

"What are they going to charge? I can't afford . . ."

"We'll earn our keep here, I promise. You won't be out anything for room and board." Anna wrung her handkerchief. "Please, Ott. All my friends are here. I'm on the basketball team."

"What about you, Johnnie Ruth?" It was as if he'd only just remembered the other young girl in the room.

"I want to stay with Anna Mae."

"Well, perhaps you two should take some time. Pray about it."

Johnnie said under her breath, "You're just saying that because you hope God will tell us to do what *you* want us to."

If Arthur heard the remark, he ignored it. He pulled his pipe out of his coat pocket. After testing the depth of the tobacco with his forefinger, he bent and snapped a straw from the whisk broom on the hearth. Lighting the straw from a low flame, he drew on the pipe until he was satisfied it was lit.

"All right," he said. "I guess you two do need to stay here — for the inquest, anyway."

Anna paled. "Inquest?"

"Yeah. I imagine there'll be one. And Wooley's trial..."

"Oh." Anna felt Johnnie's arm slip around her waist. Ott looked at the girls intently.

"You know they're going to ask you about that phone call," he said.

"Yes, I know . . ." Anna's voice trailed off.

"Are you sure you've told everything you remember?"

"I'm sure, Ott."

"If you just forgot to tell Papa something, or if you misspoke . . . Well, you're just a girl. You won't get in trouble. Tell the truth."

"She's telling the truth!" Johnnie spoke sharply.

Arthur stepped back. His little sister had never spoken to him like that. Silence hung in the room among the three of them.

"All right. I'm not suggesting anything. You're my little sisters. It's my job to take care of you. I wish I knew what Papa would do."

A polite rap on the door preceded Mary McCarty's entrance into the parlor.

"I'm so sorry to disturb you, but Jim Randolph is here and has some questions about the Sheriff's belongings."

"Please tell him we'll be right along." Arthur drew deeply on his pipe.

"I will." Mary started to leave then turned. "Arthur, I hope you will allow the girls to stay with us for the rest of the term. We would love to have them."

"Yes, I think so. If you're sure it's no bother. I'm sure the girls would like that. Much obliged for asking."

"Wonderful! Well, I'll tell Jim you'll be right along."

When the parlor door had closed, Anna said, "Thank you, Ott." She gave Johnnie a nudge.

The younger girl started. "Oh, yes. Uh — thank you, Ott." Anna poked again. "And — and — I'm sorry I sassed."

Thirty-Three

The logs in the fireplace burned low yet Anna remained on the sofa — alone now since Ott left to make arrangements to move their possessions from the jail apartment. Johnnie was helping Mary McCarty put away the banquet of food brought in by friends and neighbors.

We're orphans now. She buried her face in her hands. Her shoulders shook with silent sobs.

She wasn't sure how long she sat there before she heard the door open. She reached for the damp handkerchief to dry her cheeks as best she could.

"Anna Mae?" Her heart leapt a little when she recognized Monroe's voice. "You're crying?" He moved quickly to sit beside her. "Why are you crying? Don't cry."

He slipped his arm around her. His left hand touched her cheek and gently eased her head onto his shoulder. His lips brushed the top of her dark head. "Uh, Anna, this might not be the time to talk about this, but I've got to know . . ." He paused then spoke quickly, "Gustie says you might go live with Ott!"

"M-m-m…" Sniff.

"Oh, please don't go. I have a hard time getting *here* from Ector. West Texas might as well be on the moon. I'll never make it there. If you move, I'll never see you again."

Anna raised her head. "Well, actually . . ."

"Tell you what. Let's get married. Sure. We could get married. Then you wouldn't have to move off. I know I don't have a job right now — but Mr. Babcock promised me one — starting next month."

"Monroe . . . I . . . You . . ." Anna pulled away from him and sat up straight.

"I promise you I'll take care of you. I promise no one will ever make you cry again. They make you cry — I make them cry."

Anna gave something like a laugh.

"Monroe . . ."

"I know I spend a lot of time on the band. But — I don't have to have a band. Can't support a wife playing in a band. I love you, Anna. I love you so much I can't even think of how to tell you."

Let me count the ways? And he'd give up the band? For me? For love of me?

"What do you say?" Monroe rushed on.

"Hush a minute," Anna broke in, "let me say something. First of all, I'm not going to West Texas."

Monroe threw both arms around her, kissing her squarely on the lips. A short sweet kiss.

Anna laughed. "Wait a minute. The McCartys have invited Johnnie and me to stay here until summer and finish this school term." She took his hand. "Monroe, I want to finish school. It's important to me."

"That's swell. You can finish here . Or you can finish in Ector if we get married . . ."

"I want to be an English teacher."

"You can do that. You can teach school. Or maybe we'll have a houseful of kids for you to teach things to."

"Monroe!"

He laughed, wrapped her in his arms. They cuddled on the sofa. Monroe said softly, "I'll come see you every month. I'll hop a freight to Gainesville and hitch a ride from there. When school's out you can come spend the summer with Gustie. We'll talk about it some more then. Please don't go away from me. I love you, Anna Mae Long. Please say you'll marry me."

Anna smiled. "I'm sure I'll marry you. Someday. We can talk about it more next summer."

A high school diploma or a wedding ring? A long separation

— maybe forever — from Monroe, with graduation at the end? Or happiness now with the man I love? I don't have to decide right now. . .

Her tears gone, she nestled against his shoulder. The pulse in her temple matched the one in his throat. *Two hearts beating as one?*

She sighed. "I love you, too, Monroe."

Thirty-Four

One would have reason to expect that such an event in a small town would change the lives of everyone involved. And many lives did take a new turn after of the death of Sam Long.

Jake Wooley, the bank robber, developed an infection from the shotgun blast and the shattered windshield that cut his face. The poison traveled to his brain and he died three days after Sam Long's funeral.

Virgil and Rose Wooley lost both their sons in the space of a week. After Jake's funeral, Rose calmly told Virgil that if she ever so much as smelled liquor on his breath she would leave faster than you could say 'Jack Robinson.' Virgil, not wanting to lose any more of his family, took heed. A few years later, the Wooleys, with Cora and the grandchildren, made the trek to California with other Okies trying to escape the dust bowl.

Olin McCarty was so inspired by Sam's courage on that January day, that he gave up an opportunity to play basketball for Oklahoma A&M. Instead he enrolled at the police academy in Pauls Valley. He ultimately rose to the rank of Captain with the Oklahoma State Police.

Aaron and Mary McCarty enjoyed having Anna Mae and Johnnie Ruth with them so much, they continued taking in children in need of a home. When Aaron realized Olin was not interested in the hardware business, he offered a partnership to **Floyd Hyde**.

Frank Eastham was awed by what Sam Long did. As far as he was concerned, Sam took that bullet for him. He vowed to make his life worth the sacrifice. In October, 1929, Frank was able to save the bank by using his own wealth to cover the losses from the stock market crash. Throughout the depression years, he continued to help the poor farmers, enlisting consultants from A&M to test the soil, establishing a rent-free Farmer's Market on the square, and encouraging the barter system throughout the town. When the bank was forced to repossess a farm, Frank immediately leased it to the former owner for a reasonable and fair share of the crops.

Sarah Eastham was so distraught when Frank emptied their bank accounts, she left Marietta for an extended visit to her sister in Tulsa. She never came back to Love County. There was gossip she met and married an oil man, but no one really knew. And few cared.

Carl and Gustie Locke. Unfortunately, Carl lost his job after the big crash of 1929. He began traveling to other states to look for work. While trying to catch a ride on a freight train, he fell onto the tracks and was killed, leaving Gustie with two young daughters, Anna Ruth and Carlene.

Johnnie Ruth went to Pampa Texas with her brother Arthur and graduated from high school with honors. There she met and married a young teacher named Jimmy Milsap. They raised a family and 'lived happily ever after.'

Wendell Allen and Mattie Lou Hudson. After Sarah Eastham left town, Mattie hired out to care for sick folks Doctor Autry referred to her. Wendell held onto his job at Gaines Dairy through good times and bad, finally being promoted to supervisor. After four years of sitting together in church and holding hands behind the songbook, Mattie Lou agreed to marry Wendell Allen. She never gave up on her dream of finishing high school. She answered a magazine advertisement for LaSalle Extension University, a correspondence school, and graduated in 1948. The same year her oldest daughter, LouAnna Allen, was valedictorian of Marietta High School.

Inez Jenksinson. Indeed, one might hope that such a dramatic event would change one's life and attitude, but I have to report that Inez Jenkinson did not change. Not one whit.

Anna Mae Long and Monroe Alderson. When Anna visited Gustie the next summer, Monroe wooed his young sweetheart earnestly. They were married on August 28, 1928. Music became a recreational pastime for Monroe, and throughout the years the Alderson house was the gathering place for amateur musicians. Monroe may have stopped performing in public, but he never stopped entertaining. The six children who came along were taught by Monroe to sing harmony and by Anna to speak sentences that were grammatically correct.

From time to time, Anna thought of the telephone conversation that factored so heavily in the events of that January day. She would struggle with guilt and grief, wondering what she might have done differently. Comfort finally came through her faith in God's merciful grace and his ability to make all things new. She knew in her heart that Sam had not held her responsible.

Anna and Monroe remained sweethearts the rest of their lives. Anna's love for poetry continued. Edgar A. Guest, 'The People's Poet', was a favorite, but she always felt the words of Robert Browning best described her life with Monroe: "Grow old along with me. The best is yet to be."

At the celebration of their 50th wedding anniversary in 1978, Monroe swung Anna around in a big hug and said to the crowd of family and friends, "I can't believe I talked this pretty little girl into marrying me!"

A happy and contented life is often nothing more than many ordinary days strung together. Those times give us the courage and strength to handle the extraordinary. Thank God for ordinary days.

An Interview with Dot Hatfield

1. What inspired this story?

Sam Long was my grandfather; my mother was Anna Mae. This is a family story I heard from my mother as a child when I asked about my grandparents. As I got older I learned a few more details. My mother and my Uncle Sam Long each wrote a narrative about the bank robbery to be included in a history of Love County. The scene in the bank is almost verbatim what my grandfather, before he died, told Anna and her brother Sam.

2. What/Where is truth?

I'm not sure I want to sort truth from fiction in this story even if I had space. I hope readers will enjoy is for what it is, fiction based on truth.

3. What is your message? Who speaks for you? What would you like readers to glean and take away?

That the strength and wisdom we gain from ordinary days sustains us during the extraordinary. We should enjoy the ordinary days for the peace and stability they represent.

Also, I wanted very much to honor my mother in this story. My parents had a loving – and fun – relationship. This story touched on only the beginning of their time together, but I wanted to show something of what they had.

4. Authors are deliberate and intentional. Did you agonize over any decisions?

The most deliberate decision was how much fiction to insert amongst the truth. There were many details I didn't know and many characters I had to invent to round out the story. Whether to use real names or not was a major decision. I finally decided only the Long/Alderson family members and the hero Olin McCarty would have their real names used.

5. What did you know up front/what was settled — and what evolved as you began to write?

I knew the details of the telephone call and the bank robbery, much of the rest is fiction and evolved as I wrote and explored each character's motivation. That's why it's a novel based on a true story rather than creative non-fiction.

6. Did you already know the ending when you began writing?

Of course I knew Sam died of his wounds but I actually toyed with the idea of a "happier" ending. When the narrative developed into Anna's story, I discarded that idea. Anna was who she was because of what happened to her when she was young.

7. Your books don't usually contain swear words. What made you decide to allow Sam and Jake Wooley to swear?

Hoping to be accurate. From the stories I've heard, my grandfather was a Christian, respectful of women and protective of young folk. But an expletive he used often was "Hell." As I said, the words he said to the robber and the fact that the thief stood over Sam and cursed him are factual. It didn't seem to me a man like Jake Wooley would say "Gee Whiz."

8. How do you begin writing? Do you have snippets of ideas and information that you weave together, or do you begin in a linear fashion?

I write mostly in a linear fashion and usually the first draft is hand written. I edit as I type into the computer. Although writers are usually advised against this, I need to have a chapter pretty clean before I can move on to the next plot line. Sometimes in the final editing I feel the need to backtrack and insert a chapter to clarify a point in the story. If I need to rewrite at that time at least I'm not dealing with typos and grammar errors.

9. Which is more difficult for you as a writer — the beginning or the end? What about in this particular story?

In nearly all my stories the most difficult part is the ending. I always have an idea of the outcome of the story, but the exact ending is never clear until I'm there.

10. Authors conduct research, even when writing fiction. What kinds of things did you research for this story?

Most of the research involved in An Ordinary Day was with the intent of being authentic to the times. I researched cars, electric starters on automobiles, Drip-o-lators and Monitor Top refrigerators. I was careful to stay in the late 1920's with the descriptions. I also researched the newspaper accounts of the bank robbery. The librarian in Marietta was extremely helpful in tracking down these documents. I needed to know if what I remembered of my conversations with my mother was in line with what was reported at the time. And it was.

11. How long did it take you to write this?

I started in 2011 – so, that's two years for writing and editing. That seems like a long time but there were times I really got stuck and had my doubts about finishing. This book probably had the longest editing time of anything else I've written. I did more re-writing than ever before on a project.

12. Do you write continually until it is finished — or do you leave the writing for a while and then return?

There will be periods when I'm not actually writing on the manuscript, but I'm usually thinking about it and researching ideas.

13. What other possible endings were considered?

A fictional ending where Sam recovered from his wounds. Also, I thought of ending the book with the funeral chapter and the quote from John… "Greater love hath no man than this …"

14. What is your favorite part of the story?

I enjoyed writing the side story about Mattie and Wendell. Telling about their relationship was a good break from some of the tenser scenes.

15. What was the hardest part of writing this story? What were some of your personal conflicts?

The scenes involving my mother, Anna — with Sam, with her ailing mother or my dad, Monroe. She was such a tender, loving person and I wanted to convey that trait in her even when she was a girl. I had only my imagination as a resource for how it was for Anna during that time.

16. Why did you choose this title? What were some of the other possibilities you considered?

This was always my working title and I could just never come up with anything better. The idea is that it was An Ordinary Day that became extraordinary.

17. What is next? Do you have any other stories in mind, waiting to be written?

I can work on only one project at a time, but I always have something on the back burner of my brain.

Acknowldegements

Writing a book is much like having a child. It seems to take forever to be born. Often thinking of a name is difficult. And it takes a village to help get it right.

Thank you to my critique group, Central Arkansas Writers (Dorothy Johnson, Pat Laster, Freeda Nichols and Rhonda Roberts), for their assistance in all aspects of making this story come together, from first idea to finished project.

Thanks to Steve May and Karis Alderson for creative editing suggestions and to Betty Liddle for copy editing the final draft. I'm forever grateful to Steve May for the formatting, cover design and publishing skills he provided.

A great contribution came from narratives written by Anna Mae Long Alderson and Samuel Francis Long and published in the book *Love County History Book*, circa 1985.

I am indebted to Niki Powell, Love County Librarian, who made newspaper accounts from the

Marietta Herald, Marietta Monitor, Gainesville (TX) Daily Register and the Daily Ardmoreite available.

Thanks to Greg Moore, Literacy Specialist at Wilbur D. Mills Education Service Cooperative, who developed the *Interview with Dot Hatfield.* Greg is a co-worker, friend and encourager.

Finally, I appreciate the support I have felt from my family as I fictionalized a true story that belongs to all of us.

Musical and poetic references: *A Cup of Coffee, A Sandwich and You* written by Billy Rose, Al Dubin, Joseph Meyer; *Ragtime Cowboy* Joe written by Grant Clarke, Lewis F. Muir and Maurice Abrahams; *I'd Love to Live in Loveland With a Girl Like You* written by W.R. Williams; *Love Lifted Me* written by James Rowe; *Bringing in the Sheaves* written by Knowles Shaw; *I'm in Love With You, Honey* by Haven Gillespie, Seymour Simons, Richard Whiting; *Sonnets from the Portuguese #43, How Do I Love Thee* by Elizabeth Barrett Browning; *I Had a Wooden Whistle*, author unknown; *Rabbi Ben Ezra*, by Robert Browning.

For more information on Dot Hatfield,
visit dothatfield.com

15996413R00117

Made in the USA
San Bernardino, CA
14 October 2014